SHADOWS

Stories with a Supernatural Twist

Anne Goring

CHIVERS

British Library Cataloguing in Publication Data available

This Large Print edition published by AudioGO Ltd, Bath, 2013.
Published by arrangement with the Author

U.K. Hardcover ISBN 978 1 4713 2962 3
U.K. Softcover ISBN 978 1 4713 2963 0

Printed and bound in Great Britain by
TJ International Limited

CONTENTS

MRS VOGEL'S GHOST

Mrs Vogel died, as she lived, an embittered woman. Life, she insisted, had been unfair to her. She had been the constant target of Other People wishing to impede her progress along Life's Way. Death was no exception.

'Your fault,' Mrs Vogel gasped to her daughter Vivvy, turning purple as her over-burdened system finally gave up. 'Too rich . . . too many currants . . . how many times have I told you . . . Oh, the pain . . .'

So, seriously annoyed and frustrated (she was just about to sneak a look at the last page of the detective story she was reading to discover the identity of the strangler) she died at the age of eighty-nine due, she believed, to an excess of dried fruit in a cake baked traitorously in her own kitchen.

Blaming Vivvy, as usual, to the last.

*   *   *

'Feeling guilty is part of the natural progress of grieving,' said the doctor, paying a rushed courtesy call a couple of weeks after the funeral. 'You did everything you could and more besides. Your mother wasn't an easy woman to deal with. I think you coped splendidly. Put it behind you now. Take up

1

new interests. Evening classes . . . a long holiday—Torquay's nice at this time of year—charities are always crying out . . . Good grief, is that the time? I've six more calls to make . . .'

Vivvy closed the door on the doctor's harassed back and stared thoughtfully down the gloomy hall. She was not aware that she had spoken of guilt. Or of how to fill her time now Mother no longer occupied most of it. The doctor had attributed these normal reactions to her quite arbitrarily. She was grateful. How could she have told him the truth? One should not feel gloriously, overwhelmingly released at the decease of one's sole remaining parent. It was not seemly.

Vivvy walked down the narrow dark hall to the narrow dark kitchen. In this last year when Mother had been confined upstairs and unable to criticise, Vivvy had made one or two hopeful attempts to brighten the sullen decor. But the new flowery curtains and bright rug stood out too garishly against the dingy brown cabinets and elderly cooker.

'It will all have to go,' she said cheerfully. 'I shall have a new fitted kitchen. All white, with perhaps a hint of lemon. Dishwasher, automatic washing machine, fridge-freezer, double glazing and a porch—no, a conservatory over the back door. No nasty draughts then and somewhere to put my geranium cuttings in the winter. Oh, and a nice

2

warm radiator once I've got the central heating in . . .'

'Don't count your chickens,' said Mother, from the plastic urn on the kitchen cabinet. 'You've not found the will yet.'

'The will doesn't really matter,' Vivvy said. 'Everything will come to me eventually. There's no other living relative that I know of.'

'Hold things up, though, won't it?' Mother said. 'Solicitors will have a field day. It could go on for years.'

Vivvy regarded the plastic container with distaste. It was unsettling to hear Mother's voice so clearly. Even more unsettling after dark when Mother loomed and faded in unexpected corners.

The first time it happened, the night of the funeral, Vivvy had been cosily tucked up in bed with a box of Belgian chocolates, a glossy magazine and late night easy listening on the radio. She thought at first that the sight of her mother's familiar whiskery jaw and glaring eyes hovering above the foot of the bed was an illusion brought on by the two stiff whiskeys with which she had restored herself after enduring the necessary rites at the crematorium. Then she took in the ethereal silvery garments lifting and floating and twining about Mother's ample shape. She would never have dared to create an illusion so unsuitably dressed.

'Mother? Is that you?' Vivvy quavered, a

3

half-eaten vanilla truffle slipping from her fingers.

'Who else would it be?' Mrs Vogel snarled, swelling into a massive presence through which the figured walnut wardrobe doors could be clearly seen.

'That . . . that garment,' Vivvy said faintly. 'Not quite . . . well, you were always one for wool next to the skin . . .'

'What I'm wearing is neither here nor there,' said Mrs Vogel. 'Now, you listen to me, my girl . . .'

'Could never even persuade you into a brushed nylon nightie.'

'There's more important matters for you to attend to than mithering about my frock! You've no right to be lying there with both bars of the electric fire on and me scarcely cold in my grave.'

'Hot, Mother,' Vivvy corrected. 'You specified cremation, on account of detesting worms.'

'Stop splitting hairs! You know what I mean. It's the irreverence that's so offensive. Chocolates! This month's WITH-IT WOMAN! Radio 2! You should be mourning my passing in a decent fashion. Weeping into your pillow or pacing the floor, hollow-eyed with lack of sleep or making yourself endless cups of tea.'

'I managed a few tears at the crem,' said Vivvy, 'but I think it was the carnations setting

4

off my hay fever. I've slept very well since I haven't had to listen out for you having one of your turns. And I've not had a cup of tea since you . . . er, passed on. I always preferred coffee but you took umbrage at the smell. I didn't like to upset you more than necessary.'

Mrs Vogel swelled again, her transparent bosom advancing monstrously over the candlewick bedspread, the whiskers on her jaw thrusting forward so belligerently that Vivvy, fearing she might be impaled on the longest and sharpest, snatched up WITH-IT WOMAN and held it prudently between herself and her ghostly parent.

'Just remember, my girl,' Mrs Vogel hised. 'This is my house. Everything in it belongs to me.'

'Did, Mother,' Vivvy protested. 'Not now. How can it when you're de . . . you've passed away? Besides, I'm entitled to make myself a bit more comfortable here. I think you owe me that for all the years I've spent looking after you. I mean, you wouldn't part with a penny unless it was for your own comfort, so there's a nice little nest egg to add to the mingy bit I managed to save.'

Mrs Vogel bared her ghostly dentures in an unpleasant smirk. 'Ah, passed away I might have, thanks to you and your currants. But not passed on, if you take my meaning. Far too much to keep an eye on here. I could never rest easy anywhere else knowing that you'd be making all manner of changes and upsets in my house if I didn't put a stop to it. I know you, you see. A poor weak vessel. You take after your father. I had to be firm with him, just like I was with you. He'd never have died a hero's death if I hadn't put backbone into him. I mean, look at you now. Reading dirty books with half-naked women on the cover and clogging your arteries with over-rich food and I haven't been gone a week.'

'WITH-IT WOMAN's a perfectly respectable journal,' Vivvy said. 'Wouldn't suit you, of course. More into Carefree Co-habiting and How to Achieve Astounding Orgasms, than Ten Tasty ways with Leftover Cauliflower.'

'Disgusting!' Mrs Vogel snapped. 'And what's more I don't care for your tone. I didn't bring you up to cheek your elders.'

Vivvy prevented herself from flinching. She swallowed back the meek conciliatory words that automatically sprang to her lips. Her mother was dead. Dead! She might have been under Mother's thumb in life, but she had no intention of being browbeaten by her bullying shade.

'Take that look off your face,' said Mrs Vogel. 'I won't have defiance. Just remember that I'll be watching. Whatever tricks you get up to I'll know all about it.'

With that final sally she disappeared in a gust of icy air that set the wardrobe doors

6

rattling and shivered the curtains.

*   *   *

'Stop standing there looking half-soaked and talking rubbish about kitchens,' said Mrs Vogel jerking Vivvy out of her reverie. 'You know my wishes. Put me in my Final Resting Place. Reunite me with Your Poor Father.'

Vivvy sighed. It seemed unkind not to grant Mother's last request. Besides, Mother might feel grateful enough to give up this ridiculous haunting.

She picked up the plastic urn and carried it to the sitting room. For as long as she could remember the shelf in the corner alcove had been dedicated to her father, The Hero. On it stood a large photograph of her parents arm-in-arm at their wedding, a smaller photograph of her father in wartime RAF uniform, a vase of dried flowers and an ornamental brass urn containing her father's ashes.

Vivvy had only the sketchiest memory of her father. She remembered laughter, though. A commodity singularly absent at home after his demise. She remembered how secure her small paw had felt in his big fist. Not that he was a large man. In civvies beside his hefty wife in her shoulder-padded, box-pleated wedding costume he looked almost weedy, looking up at her in a timidly loving way. Though the grinning LAC in the other photograph had

7

a cocky look, as though Mrs Vogel—or the RAF—really had taught him a thing or two.

He had been killed, not in some corner of a foreign field but at a barrage balloon site in East Anglia during a hit and run raid.

'Sacrificed in defence of his country,' Mrs Vogel was wont to sigh. 'If only I had been at his side in his Moment of Valour.'

Vivvy was proud of her father who had rescued an injured woman from a blazing building before being felled by a toppling chimney. She basked in the reflected glow of his valour through her solitary childhood, her growing-up years and the dull, dead end jobs that kept her close to home and Mother, who was likely to be overcome with innumerable strange and painful symptoms if Vivvy so much as gently tugged the apron strings.

Mrs Vogel's regime had ensured solitariness. She had strong views on child-rearing, with much emphasis on high moral standards, filial obedience and protection from corrupting outside influences, which included unsuitable friendships and too much useless education. Mrs Vogel perfected her own personal career of hypochondria in early middle age. Thereafter Vivvy never had a moment to call her own and was eventually forced to give up work in order to pander to Mrs Vogel's every whim.

In Vivvy's childish imagination, her father's brave deed put him on a par with the saints

8

and angels pictured in the improving books which was all she was allowed to read on long, tedious Sundays. Sometimes she even imagined that there was a shadowy overlay on the photograph, a hint of long white robes, feathery wings, a shimmering halo.

He had been her model. Whenever rebellion rose in her frustrated heart, she thought of Dad dying a hero's death. She could never have let him down by turning her back on what was clearly her duty; to look after her ageing and infirm parent. If sacrifice were needed, then sacrifice it would have to be. She owed him no less. She felt guilty for feeling from time-to-time that his heroism was something of a burden. She closed her mind to the pursuit of imaginary avenues of what might have been had her father not been such a shining example.

'There you are then, Mother,' she said, setting the plastic urn beside the brass one. 'I hope that suits you. And you, Dad. Reunited at last,' she added, casting a cautious glance around the apparently empty room and adding to herself, 'And I hope that's the end of all this haunting nonsense.'

*   *   *

The house remained so peaceful for the next few days that Vivvy truly thought that Mother was laid to rest.

She kept an appointment with the solicitor. Mother's gloomy prognostications about delays were reinforced by the solicitor's reassurances. He was doing all within his power to facilitate matters, but one had to be thorough. The law did not allow for short cuts. If there had been a properly-drawn up and witnessed will, of course, that would have put a totally different complexion on the matter.

The solicitor smiled encouragingly. His teeth were shiny white, like polished bone. Whenever she visited him she felt that she had been mentally chewed up, crunch, crunch, by those sharp teeth then spat out again.

To dispel the feeling of being an insignificant and helpless mouthful she comforted herself by visiting the shopping mall. She slid into bed that night with an armful of catalogues from the travel agent, the kitchen equipment shop, the furniture emporium. The future glowed at her from the glossy, coloured pages. Comfortable armchairs, shiny-topped units, tropical paradises . . . She drifted to sleep while browsing through a catalogue of white-utilities . . .

She awoke in a cold sweat.

The dream had been so clear, so full of loud shouting voices that she might have been watching a film on television.

There were three people in her dream. Mother was there, solid and vigorous and young, as she had been in the wedding photograph. She was clutching the arm of her bridegroom. Father was dressed in RAF uniform and onto his other arm clung a young woman Vivvy didn't know. A pretty, blue-eyed slip of a thing, with piled up blonde hair.

The three of them appeared to be standing in the aisle of a packed cinema. Behind them flickered a black-and-white film, cigarette smoke coiled like white snakes in the searchlight beam from the projection room, people followed the usherette's torch to their seats. But the three were too busy arguing to notice. Their mouths opened and shut, fists were shaken. Vivvy couldn't catch the words for the crackle and boom of the voices from the screen and bursts of laughter from the audience. But Mother, larger and more vociferous than the other two seemed to be winning the argument. With a sudden droop of the shoulders the blonde woman's grip slipped from father's arm, she began to drift backwards down the slope of the aisle . . .

The picture clicked off and she was awake.

It seemed extraordinarily quiet in the bedroom after the noise of the dream. The cheese-on-toast she'd had for supper, Vivvy thought, her heart pounding. And the strain of the last weeks. Bound to be some sort of reaction.

'Vivvy! Vivvy, love,' said an anguished male voice in her ear. 'You've got to help.'

11

'What?' Vivvy jerked her head round in time to catch the faintest, wavering, transparent shape hovering beyond the glow of the bedside light.

'Can't stop . . . can't manage . . . never practised, see. Just try your best, love. Get her off my back . . . off yours, too. I'll tell you how . . .'

'Don't listen to him!' Mother's ethereal form loomed beside the bed. A beefy transparent arm swiped at the other apparition which instantly disappeared, an expression of anguish remaining fractionally after the rest of the wavering shape had gone. 'I'll be with you in half a tick, Stan,' she bellowed. 'I just want a word with our Vivvy.'

'Mother, whatever's going on? Was that—?'

'Your dear father, My Hero,' said Mrs Vogel, the steely light in her ghostly eyes contradicting the beatific smile that showed a set of tombstone teeth. Not dentures. Only the merest hint of a black whisker on her chin. Dark hair, Marcel-waved into artificial ridges. Even a hint of shoulder pads under the ethereal streamers of her robe.

'Why, Mother,' said Vivvy. 'You look different.'

'In my prime,' said Mrs Vogel. 'That's how it works over here.' She glared disdainfully down her fleshy nose at Vivvy. 'Pity you took after your father's side. Wishy-washy lot. Not only in looks, either.' She shook her head grimly. 'Stan's gone soft since I last had him in hand. Never mind, I'll soon knock him into shape again. . His trouble is that he doesn't know what's best for him.'

'And you do?' quavered Vivvy.

'Most certainly. Like I've always done for you. So think on, my girl, if he starts bellyaching just shut your ears.' Her voice echoed hollowly from the landing. 'Even if you can't see me, I'm watching. Just remember, I'll know if you and him get up to mischief.'

Vivvy thumped down crossly under the bedclothes. To be haunted by one parent was bad enough. But two! Would she never be able to call the autumnal years of her life her own?

*   *   *

She stared at her father's photograph long and hard the next day. Was it imagination or was the cocky look she knew so well somewhat diminished. Was there the hint of a frown? A droop to the mouth? She was sure that the halo of light round his head was brighter, the feathery tracery of wings at his back a little more clearly delineated.

Maisie

The name came clearly into her head. At the same moment the face of the blonde young woman of her dream flashed across her inner eye.

Talk to Maisie. She'll know what to do.

13

Quick. She's in the shelter in the park.

I'm going potty, she thought, banging the front door on her way out. Seeing things. Hearing voices. None of this is happening at all. I'm having a nervous breakdown. Why else am I doing this?

The rain blew horizontally against her umbrella as she walked three times round the deserted bowling green. Eventually she plucked up courage enough to edge into the shelter by the duck pond.

Maisie, all soulful blue eyes and tumbling blonde hair shimmered in the darkest corner.

Vivvy slowly closed her umbrella, sighed and sat down.

'As nervous breakdowns go,' she said, 'this one takes some beating.'

'You're not having a nervous breakdown, love,' said the apparition, earnestly. 'And both me and your dad's right sorry we've got to get you mixed up in our affairs but we can't see any other way. It's your mother, you see, now she's crossed to our side. She's that strong willed she'll turn poor Stan into a real hero against his better judgement. Then it'll be upstairs for him—harp, halo, eternal bliss, the lot. And what sort of boring fate is that for any normal hot-blooded man, let alone woman, I ask you?'

'Please don't ask,' said Vivvy wearily. 'Just explain.'

Ten minutes later she walked back home, her thoughts scurrying about like a nestful of disturbed ants. All these years she had tried to live up to her father's heroic reputation, a reputation that was nothing but a fairytale dreamed up by her mother. He hadn't died on the barrage balloon site in a gallant act of rescue, but had breathed his last during a Three Stooges film on the back row of the pictures in a moment of over-excitement with Maisie.

'Proper romantic,' Maisie sighed dreamily. 'A heart attack. And not surprising the naughty things he got up to. Oh, but I did miss him. I suppose that's what made me a bit forgetful. I stepped off the pavement right under a tram a month later. We've been happy as larks ever since. At least until your mother put in an appearance. A right killjoy she is.' Maisie's blue eyes were sympathetic. 'Makes me realise what a life you must have had, you poor thing. If only your dad hadn't had his dicky heart that no-one suspected, things would've been very different. We planned to make it all legal after the war and take you to live with us in a nice bungalow by the sea.'

Vivvy didn't take off her coat when she got

15

in. She found a shopping bag, picked up the two urns, packed her nightie and a change of underwear, checked that she'd got enough money in her purse and walked back down the hall.

Mother materialised, guarding the front door like an elephantine see-through barrier.

'Where do you think you're going?' she shrieked, Marcel waves bouncing in agitation. 'I know what you've got in your bag. I forbid you to remove my ashes from this house!'

'I've been the victim of emotional blackmail all my life,' Vivvy said sternly. 'You've always twisted the truth to suit yourself, I can see that now. You reckoned you always knew best for me—but it was really what was best for you. I've had enough of it. All that about Dad was a load of codswallop . . .'

'This is my home!'

'Was,' Vivvy said, stepping forward briskly. 'Time you had a change.'

It was an odd sensation passing through a transparent person. An instant of being enfolded by what felt like jellified ice all the while being bombarded by tangling chaotic emotions of impotent rage, aggression and spite flashing red and warlike . . . then she was through to the other side.

Vivvy swept down the street feeling oddly young and lighthearted. As though she was reborn. As perhaps she was. That moment of icy passage through Mother's spectral shape signifying a cleansing rebirth.

She was weary by the time she returned two days later to the dark house. Her house. She could feel the difference. It was waiting for her and her alone, comforting as the cup of cocoa she made as soon as she'd kicked off her shoes. Hers to do what she liked with now. No argument. No having to listen to the solicitor shedding metaphorical crocodile tears on her behalf.

Mother's will , hidden by her so long ago, had been neatly tucked inside the urn that held her father's ashes. It had fallen out as she scattered ashes around Maisie's overgrown headstone in the corner of a neglected municipal graveyard on the south coast . . .

The Hero had come up trumps in the end.

*   *   *

Disposing of Mother's ashes was trickier. It involved much changing of trains and ferries and a final trip in a hired boat. Fortunately the weather was exceptionally calm. These waters, open to every Atlantic gale, were notoriously stormy. The small island where the skipper deposited her promising to come back in an hour, was perfect.

'I thought you might be in need of a new hobby, Mother,' Vivvy said when she had finished her task. 'Bird watching'll take your mind off things. Lots of them about here. They probably won't mind being bossed about a bit. But if you get bored well . . . perhaps you'll decide to pass on properly and in a dignified fashion instead of hanging around down here and making a nuisance of yourself.'

The low moaning sound wafting over the tussocky grass as Vivvy made her way back to where the boat waited was surely, she thought, straightening her shoulders and raising her chin, the call of one of the many gulls that had made this scrap of storm-wracked rock their home.

*   *   *

From time to time, reclining in her cosy, peaceful sitting room after a session at the gym or a ballroom dancing lesson or a trip to Majorca or Mexico or Malaysia, Vivvy will select a vanilla truffle from the selection of Belgian chocolates at her elbow, pour herself a glass of sherry and switch on the television.

If there happens to be a showing of an old wartime film involving heroic airmen she'll raise her glass and wink.

She never watches nature programmes.

WISH UPON A STAR

It was a dark place, a deep, dank overgrown hollow in the centre of the wood. He'd named it The Bone Pit after Miss Ellis told them about the dinosaurs. That was when the diggers first started gouging into the hillside for the new bypass and the lumpy, stone-like fossils came up with the sticky yellow clay. A professor or somebody had come from London, and there'd even been a bit on the telly about it. Miss Ellis had been quite excited.

'Think of it, children. Where the houses and the church and the railway station are now was once a steaming swamp full of enormous creatures.'

She'd reeled off a list of names he couldn't remember and pinned up pictures on the walls. He'd stared at them when he should have been doing sums. The ridge-backed monsters with mouths full of razor-edged, tearing teeth, the ones with long thin necks and tiny, sparrow-brained heads. The terra–somethings that flapped about on leathery wings. 'History is all down there under your feet,' Miss Ellis had cried, 'Layer upon layer of it!'

* * *

Now, in the wood he looked down at his battered trainers half-sunk in thick, wet leaf-mould. The tops of the trees whipped in the last of the gale. Down here, where the bramble-choked roots scrabbled down towards the water at the base of the pit, his ragged breathing sounded loud in the stillness.

He was thinking about death. Of the dinosaur skeletons sealed far below. Of his father.

He knuckled his eyes angrily. He wasn't a crybaby. He hadn't cried all day. Not through the phone calls, the neighbours mouthing secrets above his head and talking to him and Mam as though they were poorly. He hadn't cried when his mother did, nor during the hours when she wandered about the house ashen-faced, smiling a polite sort of smile to the people who came and went—and all the time her eyes full of black terror.

'He'll be all right,' she kept repeating. 'I know he'll be all right. We must be brave, Billy. He'd want us to be brave. We'll hear some good news soon.' And then, plaintively, turning the sick feeling in his stomach into something far worse, something that made him want to claw and bite and kick, 'Allen's coming round later. He says the forecast is better. The wind's beginning to drop. Perhaps there'll be some news by the time he gets here.'

The water in the pit stirred slowly among drink cans, herniated tyres and the remains of a mattress that sprouted rusty springs. Dead things. Broken things. Had his father been dumped like this unwanted rubbish? Discarded from the foundering oil rig for the violent sea to swallow into its cold, uncaring depths?

Why did it have to be Dad? Why couldn't it have happened when Dad was safe at home on leave? Why couldn't it have been Allen instead?

Allen was Dad's friend. He worked on the same oil rig. Dad had invited Allen and his girl friend round for a barbecue in the summer. After that, after he split up with his girl friend, he came to the house more and more. Dad said he was lonely, but then Dad was always inviting people home. He liked company. Mam complained that the house was a bear garden when he was on leave. Sometimes she got flushed and cross and said she just couldn't conjure meals out of thin air for every Tom, Dick and Harry he felt sorry for. But Dad just laughed and said, 'Are you calling me a bear?' And lifted her off her feet and hugged her and rubbed his bristly chin over her face until she screeched and her crossness changed to giggles.

Billy had grinned too, because anyone could see his Dad was nothing like a bear. He was a lion, his Dad. Tanned and golden-haired and unafraid. King of the jungle.

But there *was* a bear. A plump, bushy-bearded grizzly with big, hard paws always

21

filled with presents: bottles of wine, chocolates, some new toy that he thought in his jolly way, that Billy might like. Camouflage.

'Allen's so kind. Too generous for his own good,' Mam said.

'A great mate,' Dad said. 'Pity that girl of his swanned off. He doesn't say much but I reckon he's cut up about it. Well, we'll do what we can to cheer him up, won't we, love?'

Only Billy knew the truth about the bear. He alone seemed to notice that the smile never quite reached the small black eyes—eyes that were forever restless, darting, calculating, greedy. They watched Dad with an unpleasant, superior sort of glint. They watched Billy with wary contempt. But most of all they watched Mam. And then they glistened like cold, slithery pebbles; and the fingers on the big, hairy paws wove themselves tightly together until the knuckles stood sharp and white and shining against the skin.

The thick mass of grey cloud above the valley was beginning to thin. Pale shafts of sunlight filtered through the leafless branches. An iridescence coiled along the oily surface of The Bone Pit. Black reflections shifted uneasily in a downdraught of air. Billy shivered. He ought to go. He'd stayed out too long. Mam had enough to worry about. He shouldn't be here at all, anyway. He should be back at the house with the hushed-voice neighbours and the cups of tea.

And Allen.

Allen-Allen-Allen. The creaking branches caught the echo of his thoughts and flung them about. *Allen-Allen-go-away-never-come-back-any-other-day*. He put his hands over his ears, but the wood still hummed its song in his head.

The wood knew everything. Miss Ellis had told them it was very old and had once been a gigantic forest full of wolves and wild bear. Then men began to tear out the trees to make room for their crops and their cows and sheep. They needed timber for houses and barns, for ships that carried them on voyages of discovery. They needed space for villages and towns and cities. Long centuries nibbled and gnawed at it until it was only a scrap of thing, roughly triangular in shape, at the foot of the hill, crisscrossed with trails made by people and dogs and children. On one side the redbrick houses pressed up against it, his own houses closest of all. Above it was the railway cutting; below, the raw yellow gash which would be the new road by next summer.

His mother grumbled about the noise and the mud that the lorries trailed up the lane past their house on the way to the dump. But Billy stood in the garden watching them pass, thinking of the dinosaur bones that nobody had spotted, now trapped in their broken loads. He liked the idea of dinosaurs secretly and invisibly passing his house. Sometimes, under cover of the noisy lorry engines he called goodbye to them as they went on their way to a different burial ground.

The dinosaurs were older than the wood, of course. Much older and far, far deeper than the roots of the trees could reach. Perhaps if the water at the bottom of the pit had been clear he might have spotted a claw or a tooth or a bony knuckle. He could have climbed down there dead easy, fished it out and taken it to show Miss Ellis. He'd be on telly, then. Mam would boast about him to the neighbours. Dad would be right proud and give him extra pocket money.

The sudden pain doubled him over. He clutched his arms tight around his ribs, wailing aloud, 'Dad! Dad! You can't leave us, Dad!'

His foot slid in the leaf-mould against the edge of the pit, sending a cascade of dead leaves and earth into the water. For a few trembling seconds he thought he might follow. He swayed on the brim, flinging his arms wide in an effort to balance. A pebble spurted from under his scrabbling trainer. Then his feet found purchase and his body steadied.

The pebble hit the water with a thunk. Ripples rainbowed outwards, splintering the reflection of his own frightened face. The watery sun fastened on the pebble as it lodged in the muck, a tiny glimmering, bone-white circle—no, not a circle. The disturbed water distorted the image into sharp points and facets.

Billy blinked. It was only a small grey pebble, he knew; but somehow in those filthy, stained waters it sparkled with the intensity of a diamond, a snowflake, a star.

The tree branches sighed and snapped. *Wish-wish-wish-wish.*

His mind churned. People threw money into wishing wells, didn't they? And wishes were granted. That was just a pebble, but sometimes things that looked like pebbles were really fossil bones. And a dinosaur bone was surely more valuable, *stronger*, than any rotten tenpee coin.

Dinosaur. The picture swam in front of him. The one on the wall at school.

Pterodactyl. He saw it spelled out in big black letters.

'I wish . . .' he whispered.

He saw the leathery wings, the huge scaly feet as the monster flapped from the cliff edge. He saw it skimming the surface of the sea, the grey spumey breakers reaching up to snare it, but it flapped on to where the rubber life-raft lollopped up and down in the waves. He saw his father's bright head dulled by the wet, his face white and drawn, his body sagging, his eyes closed. Billy held his breath.

'No, Dad, no!' he screamed silently, 'You mustn't be dead. We need you.'

But as the leathery wings flopped and flapped above him, as the great scaly talons reached to snatch him from the dinghy, the

25

man slowly lifted his head and opened his eyes. He looked straight at Billy and he nodded. He was past speech but his message sang out clear and true.

Thanks, son, you did well. I'll be okay. You can go home, now.

It was gone.

Billy looked down at tyres and tin cans poking through oily water. The sun had gone behind clouds. The star—the pebble—had disappeared in the ooze.

He straightened up. His knees felt funny and his head was swimmy, like it had been when he had chickenpox last year. The trees still creaked and sighed. The wood was the same as it had been.

But something had changed.

He turned from the pit and began to run home along the twisty, beaten track through the wood, only stopping when he came to where the trees thinned and he could see his house. A red MG was parked in the lane outside the front gate. Allen had arrived. And Billy understood then what the change meant.

The fear was gone.

His stomach no longer twisted with the smothering dread of those small, darting eyes, of the plump, hairy, gift-bearing paws.

Grizzly bears meant nothing to someone with dinosaurs on his side.

He climbed the fence and went in through the kitchen door, shutting it softly behind him,

26

walking in on light feet through to where faces turned to look at him—to where the clouded atmosphere, heavy with tears, folded in on him.

A couple of neighbours were perched on the settee. His mother was curled in a chair like a small broken doll. Billy wanted to shout at her that she could stop crying. Dad was okay. The pterodactyl had rescued him. But he mustn't . . . couldn't. And in any case, Allen leapt up the minute he walked in and bent over Mam, taking her small hands into his big ones. Caressing her palm with his thumb, saying gently, 'I'll be away an hour at most, Claire. Then I'll come back and stay all evening. I can kip down on the settee if necessary. You mustn't be alone.'

Mum's mouth trembled. 'So kind, Allen,' she murmured. 'Thank you.' She gazed unseeingly about her. 'You're all so kind. I don't know what I'd have done without you.'

Allen came over to Billy on his large quiet bear's feet.

'Billy'll see me out, won't you, sonny?'

'I'm not your son,' Billy muttered.

Allen ruffled Billy's hair with his plump hand. Billy jerked his head away and regarded him with sullen scorn.

Allen's white teeth flashed in a smile. His gaze darted restlessly round the room while his hand moved down to fasten itself on Billy's shoulder. Billy found himself propelled out

27

into the hall in a rush.

Allen's smiled faded abruptly.

'You cheeky little sod,' he hissed. 'Don't think I haven't noticed your attitude. You need a bloody good hiding. Your mother's too soft with you, by half.'

Billy wriggled. 'Gerroff, you're hurting me.'

'I'd hurt you a bloody sight more if you were mine.'

'But I'm not, am I?' Billy said. He didn't care any more. He wasn't frightened any more. There was no reason to be. 'You're not my Dad. And when my Dad comes back I'll tell him you hurt me and he'll thump you, you'll see!'

Fingers bit through the thick wool of his sweater, digging into muscle. Billy squirmed, tears of pain and anger filling his eyes.

'Your Dad?' Allen's voice was laced with contempt, his bear's eyes as slimy as the water in the Bone Pit. 'We've heard he last of him. You don't know the North Sea in winter. He wouldn't have lasted ten minutes. None of 'em would. If you're lucky they'll find a body for you to bury.' He flung Billy from him so that he fetched up against the banisters. 'So don't quote your Dad at me, sonny. You tread very carefully when you're near me from now on. That way, things'll be a whole lot easier for all of us.'

Billy didn't think any more. He threw himself at Allen, hammering at him with his fists, choking out the words, 'It's not true! He's not dead. He's been rescued. I've seen him. He's on his way home.'

Allen trapped his flailing arms in one big paw, dragged him upwards until his feet kicked wildly at the air then let him go, so that he staggered and fell backwards onto the bottom step of the staircase.

'Like I said, I'll be back in an hour,' he snarled. 'And I'll keep on coming back. Now your Dad's gone, your poor mother'll need a man to lean on. That man's going to be me. And if you go telling lies about me to your mother, there'll be worse to come for you. You'd better believe that, sonny boy.'

The door slammed behind him. Billy breathed deeply. His arms felt as though they'd been wrenched from his shoulders and painfully stuffed back any old way. But that change, that core of certainty, of strength, he'd felt in the wood was untouched and unharmed. Grizzly bears were powerful, but they didn't stand a chance against dinosaurs.

He knew what he had to do.

He raced up the stairs to his bedroom. The window overlooked the front garden and the lane. He stared down at Allen opening the gate, walking to the car.

Dinosaurs. Which one would fancy a nice juicy grizzly for a snack.

A picture on the wall, the name in big black letters.

Tyrannosaurus Rex.

A glimmer of light in oily water. A snowflake, a diamond, a star.

'I wish,' he breathed, 'I wish . . .'

He felt it first. The reverberating thump, thump of its feet, then the bellow of rage and lust as it scented its prey.

Billy turned his head to watch the wood where the lane curved against its edge. Saw the trees shake and quiver and break apart at the monster's approach. Not the leafless winter trees but richly green like enormous newly-uncurled ferns in which smaller beasts writhed and flittered.

Tyrannosaurus Rex.

It thundered from the wood, towering above the house, its great crested back obliterating the view, telegraph poles snapping like matchsticks against its armour-plated sides. With a howl of triumph it bore down on its victim.

Allen was getting into the car when he saw it.

Billy saw the expression on his face and laughed aloud.

'You see, old grizzly,' he yelled, 'you don't stand a chance against a dinosaur.'

Tyrannosaurus Rex bent its head.

The massive jaws opened. The curving teeth scooped the car up. The metal body shrieked its agony, the windscreen exploded, a limb flailed wildly before sagging loose and lifeless amid tatters of upholstery.

30

Somewhere else, away from the carnage outside, a phone rang, was instantly answered. Calmly, Billy heard his mother's distant cry. 'He's all right. Oh, thank God! Billy! The helicopter's found your Dad!'

He didn't answer. He went on staring into the wild red eye of the dinosaur until the creature lowered its head as though in obeisance and slid back, back among the tangled creeper growth of the sheltering forest.

Other cries. A slamming of doors, a scurrying of people from their houses. A voice wailing, 'That damned bypass! I knew something like this would happen. Those lorries should never have been allowed to use this lane.'

The mangled red sports car lay crushed under a fallen telegraph pole, half buried in boulders and clay. An overturned lorry blocked the roadway. The dazed driver was being helped out of the cab.

Billy let out his breath on a trembling sigh. His glance slid over the rubble. There might be dinosaur bones in that lot. He'd have a good look before they cleared it away.

Deep in the wood the foul black water at the base of the pit stirred. A gas bubble shimmered to the surface and plopped apart. Its passing caused something in the ooze to shift. Tiny points of light glinted briefly, brilliantly, in the pale sunlight, before the dark waters once more sealed it in.

THE PARTY

Mrs Paget lay in the double bed while her husband dressed. With her eyes tight-closed she saw each deliberate moment; the big coarse-nailed hands pulling, buttoning, zipping. He whistled through his teeth all the while. Presently he would go to the window, rattle the curtains aside and say, 'You're missing the best part of the day, Cora.'

Each separate noise—the grate of his slippers on the carpet, the tuneless whistle, his harsh-toned voice speaking the words she had heard with little variation each morning for nearly forty years—fell like stones into her heart.

She had been certain when she awoke that she would go, this time, to Mrs Loveday's party. Now, listening to Arnold, she doubted that she would.

'Slip out for an hour while your husband's at his gardening club,' Mrs Loveday had urged. 'You'll enjoy it. Lots of lovely people coming and the forecast's for more of the same.' She had waved her sturdy brown arm at the cloudless sky. The warm breeze pressed the scarlet cotton sundress against her overflowing braless bosom. 'There'll be a barbecue. Do say you'll come.'

'That woman's clothes are a disgrace,'

Arnold said often. 'Mutton dressed as lamb. Gives me a pain to look at her.'

Many things about Mrs Loveday gave Arnold pain. Her clothes, her noisy parties when her friends banged car doors in the small hours and called loud, laughing goodbyes, her cats, her dogs and her wild, neglected garden.

Above all, the garden.

Mrs Paget did not think that Mrs Loveday was a disgrace. From her window she watched her striding out up the lane towards the woods, or across the field behind the cottages, with her three lolloping dogs at her heels. In winter she wore jeans and bright furry sweaters. In summer, floating cotton dresses. There was something about the way Mrs Loveday walked with wide, confident steps, the way she swung her arms and whistled to her dogs that made Mrs Paget sigh wistfully. She did not, like Arnold, fume and glower when Mrs Loveday held her parties. Long after he was snoring she lay listening to the distant laughter, the beat of the music and imagined all the happy people overflowing Mrs Loveday's cottage, spilling out into the garden. Dancing, talking, getting tipsy, arguing, kissing. Living.

Sometimes there would be a barbecue or a fiery bonfire to send fragrant smoke wafting over the shrubs Mrs Loveday had allowed to grow luxuriantly between their garden and hers, topping the dividing wall now. There was always music. Somebody would strum a guitar and people would sing and stamp their feet. Mrs Paget always hoped that the flute player would be there. Whoever it was, played wonderfully. The tunes, formless and subtle, fell deliciously into Mrs Paget's mind, soothing her to contented sleep.

'That blasted woman,' Arnold would say next morning. 'Hardly closed my eyes for that damned racket. I'll get the police round one of these days, see if I don't'

'It's not so often,' Mrs Paget begged. 'Please don't make trouble, Arnold. She's such a pleasant person to talk to. She means no harm, it's just that she has so many friends.'

Arnold's eyes were round and brown and prominent. The whites were mottled with tiny red veins that seemed to swell with the force of his anger.

'How many times must I tell you not to get involved with that woman.'

'I'm not involved. I merely pass the time of day. After all, she's our only neighbour. It would be rude to ignore her.'

'Heaven knows what sort of things happen at these so-called parties. Orgies, more like.'

'They're having fun, Arnold.'

'Fun be damned. We moved to this house so we could enjoy peace and quiet. Enjoy the garden in a rural setting. It wasn't like this in Miss Harrington's day. I don't know what she was thinking about, selling her property to a merry-blasted-widow and going off into sheltered housing.

Miss Harrington had been thin and quiet and, like Arnold, had kept her garden immaculately neat.

'Well, another six months and I'll be retired and then I shall definitely do something about it.' He thrust his heavy chin forward. 'I won't have my retirement spoiled by that woman. And you're not to speak to her. Do you hear, Nora? Do you hear?'

Mrs Paget suppressed a shudder. She had thought a lot lately about Arnold's retirement. To have him here all day, every day . . .

'Yes, Arnold,' she said quietly. 'I hear you.'

But there were times when it was impossible not to speak to Mrs Loveday. It was inevitable that they should meet. At the garden gate, in the lane, in the nearby town's small shopping centre. It would have been ridiculous to refuse the offer of a lift when she was walking back from town in bad weather. Mrs Loveday drove a small, battered car decorated with stickers exhorting passers-by to Save our Forests or Free Battery Chickens. She and her friends were into conservation and were given to organising petitions which Arnold refused to sign, or demonstrating outside the town hall carrying homemade banners. The car was always untidy. Cluttered with unusual stones and seed pods she had gathered on her walks. One or other of the dogs was always with her, shedding its hair and doggy smell over the

35

upholstery and encouraging any passenger with great sloppy licks.

Mrs Loveday drove recklessly, talking in her breezy way, raising one hand, sometimes both, from the steering wheel to emphasise some point. Tossing passenger and dog alarmingly from side to side as she made sudden swerves and unexpected gear changes. Mrs Paget found these rides both frightening and exhilarating. She herself had never learned to drive.

'There's no need,' Arnold had decided, years ago. 'I take the car to work and at other times if we go out, we go out together. Seems a needless expense for you to have lessons. Besides, you'd be too nervous. I know you, you'd panic as soon as you got into heavy traffic.'

It hadn't been so bad when they lived close to a bus route. She could get to the shops and the little museum where she had a part time job for a few years until they'd changed her hours and Arnold didn't want her working at weekends. Here, there were no buses.

'It's only a twenty minute walk,' Arnold had scoffed. 'You can't have much to carry when we do a big shop once a month at the supermarket. And I grow all the veggies and fruit. I don't know what you're moaning about. And don't go on about driving lessons again.'

Arnold drove very slowly, sitting bolt upright, glaring at every other motorist. His

36

grumbling made her stomach tense. There was nothing remotely pleasurable about drives with Arnold.

Mrs Paget lay narrowly on her side of the double bed and listened to the snick of the shears as her husband made his early morning attack on the garden.

'You'll not go wrong with Arnold,' her aunt had said, speaking out of a wealth of inexperience and a desire to get rid of a responsibility thrust upon her when Nora's parents had died within a year of each other when Nora was ten. 'He's a clean-living man, with a steady job at the council. You could go a lot further and fare worse.'

At eighteen, she clung hopefully to the thought that this was the chance to change her life with someone who would love and protect her out of affection rather than duty. She'd been glad to leave school at sixteen where shy and reserved, she was overlooked by those seeking friendships. The habit of timidity became even more ingrained after a year or so in a typing pool among girls who thought her stuck up because she could not talk easily to them of fashions and pop stars. She had been flattered by the attentions of a man so much older . . . She had a headful of unshaped, romantic dreams. Mr Right had found her, just like the heroines in the romantic novels that cluttered Aunt Ellen's shelves. She believed in eternal love and happy-ever-after. And

37

in obedience to her elders. Aunt Ellen had insisted on that. As had her parents who had produced a daughter late in their married life and regarded her as an interruption to their cosy routines.

Looking back now, she could not understand what she had seen in Arnold that she had gone so willingly to share his life. Had it been gratitude that he appeared to like, rather than tolerate her? Had it been the security he offered, the chance to move away from her aunt's old house and elderly friends? Had it been his strong, masterful personality that promised she would be cared for and loved for always?

But Arnold was not a loving man. His strong will was rooted in selfishness. Where she had expected affection there had been rebuff; instead of tender gentleness there was a brusque denial of her needs and an imposition of his own

Slowly, over the years of their marriage, she felt the person she was, the spirit, the emotional being, curling smaller and smaller until it had shrunk to a hard, tight kernel within the shell that was her outer self. Somewhere locked away was the eager, romantic girl who had loved visiting art galleries and the theatre; who had longed to travel; who had yearned for children.

Arnold had desired none of these things. Arnold wanted a nice house with her in it to attend to his comfort. Arnold wanted his gardening and his gardening club and no more than a few days away in the summer because of having to arrange for his tomatoes to be watered and the lawn to be cut. And no interest in a trip abroad to somewhere sunny and warm in the winter. 'You know my stomach. Couldn't face all that foreign travel and spicy food. No, we're better off at home, all nice and cosy.'

Mrs Paget got out of bed and went to the mirror. She stared at the thin, small sallow woman in the crumpled cotton nightdress who looked back at her. She thought: I should never have married him. And was shocked. Then realised it was true. True! And the strangest thing was that it was only in the last year or so that she had started to think like that. Before, she had considered herself a lucky woman.

She had a home that she cleaned and decorated and made soft furnishings for. Arnold never begrudged anything she spent on the house or, indeed, on herself. He knew she would never throw money away on silly things . . . He paid all the bills. He rewarded her for laundering his clothes and cooking his meals and nursing him through colds by buying her sensible kitchen gadgets for birthday and Christmas.

She turned from her mirror image and went to the window.

Down in the borders Arnold was dead-heading roses.

Snick-snick-snick.

The garden was a picture of order. The dewed lawn was smooth as green enamel, shrubs pruned to symmetrical spheres and pyramids, flowers in regimental battalions turning their faces precisely in the direction Arnold had planned. Every leaf, every petal, held itself rigidly in place in case the snapping shears or the sharp pruners or the plundering hoe spied rebellion in the ranks.

Snick-snick-snick.

Then he paused, straightened and fixed his gaze on the silver birch tree by the greenhouse.

'It'll have to go,' he'd insisted last week. 'It's got far too big. Putting out far too much shade.'

'Oh, Arnold,' she'd pleaded, 'It's such a pretty tree. I love the colour of the bark . . .'

'What you on about, Nora? Look at that branch. It's right over the glass and there's another dangling over the path. No, I'll get it seen to before the winter. Then I can put another cold frame in that corner.'

Arnold distrusted trees unless they were small and produced useful fruit. Mrs Paget was surprised that the silver birch had survived so long. The others—a field maple at the front and the two other silver birches that had prettily framed the view to the fields at the back—had been given the chop soon after they

40

moved here.

She sighed. Poor old tree. Then a glimpse of something yellow in the garden next door caught her eye. Mrs Loveday was out by the bird table in a rather fetching kimono. Her dogs were leaping about woofing happily. Mrs Paget could only catch glimpses of her between the great stands of larkspur and towering pink foxgloves that spired up among the luxuriant greenery.

'I like a garden to be wild,' she had said. 'After all, what is a weed but a wild flower in the wrong place. I like to see butterflies and birds. So what if the caterpillars eat the leaves and birds steal a little fruit. There's still plenty left for me.'

'You have green fingers,' Mrs Paget had said on one of the occasions when, unknown to Arnold, she had accepted Mrs Loveday's offer of a cup of coffee. Mrs Loveday's house rioted with plants. Orange, lemon and grapefruit seedlings grown from pips, strange shaped cacti, giant geraniums and ivies draping themselves in every corner.

'My mother was the same,' she said. 'Talk to them, love them, and they'll grow for you was her motto. So I do and they do. I don't believe in a lot of nasty spraying and pruning. Everything has the right to grow and develop in its own way.'

Down in the garden Arnold had spotted something amiss. Mrs Paget, alarmed, had

41

seen it too. She struggled with the window catch, wanting to call out and distract him, but the catch was stiff and he did not hear her rapping frantically on the glass. He leaned over the netted strawberries and picked up the blackbird that was caught by its claws. With a precise movement he stopped the fluttering and tossed the bundle of feathers onto the compost heap.

Mrs Paget pressed the back of her hand against her mouth to suppress a cry of outrage.

Tried, sentenced, executed. Arnold's law.

Mrs Loveday's cat was sitting on the wall. It was the big smiling marmalade one. The pretty black cat was too nervous to stray after several traumatic encounters with Arnold. The marmalade cat was cunning and unafraid. It sat unblinking, its eyes fixed on Arnold as he progressed round the borders.

Mrs Paget was glad to see it there, so watchful and fearless. She felt encouraged by its presence, as though it were an ally. Her gaze moved on.

As though she knew she was being observed, Mrs Loveday looked up and waved. She appeared a young, sturdy figure, smiling amid the spiky flowers and greenery. Mrs Paget knew that Mrs Loveday must be at least as old as she was, but the lines under her eyes were denied by her air of vitality and the springy waves of auburn hair. Dyed, Arnold said. Did it matter? She waved back, but discreetly lest Arnold spy her at the window and be angry.

She wondered if she really dared go to the party that evening.

*   *   *

As she walked back from town later in the morning, Mrs Loveday's car squealed to a halt beside her.

'Glorious day, isn't it?' she cried. 'I've just been to the hairdressers but I'm glad to be out in the fresh air again. Oh, but you've had your hair done, too. How well it suits you.'

On impulse she had gone into a salon she normally avoided as being too smart and expensive. 'What do you suggest?' she asked timidly. 'I'd like a complete change.'

'A good cut and a few bronzy lowlights,' the young woman had said. 'Nice thick hair. Just needs updating.'

She felt very daring, but the image of the sad person she'd seen in the mirror haunted her. Someone like that would never, never defy Arnold and go to a party.

'You will try and come, won't you,' Mrs Loveday encouraged, swerving violently round a corner.

'It'll only be for an hour if I do.'

She held the plastic carrier with the new dress in it. Not at all her style, really. Too bright, too flimsy. Arnold would not like it.

She would have to hide it away.

'An hour's better than nothing,' Mrs Loveday cried. Her eyes were a twinkly green. 'And you never know, the meeting might be a long one. What time does your husband go out? Eight? Come then, before it gets too crowded. You'll not regret it.'

The phone rang when she was making a sandwich for lunch. The secretary of the gardening club was most apologetic. Would she tell Mr Paget that there was a complication about the flower show? As a committee member he'd have to stay on after the usual meeting was over to thrash out the difficulties. It looked as though it would be a lengthy business.

She put down the phone feeling that she had been given a sign. A long-unfamiliar tremor ran through her. Excitement.

Cinderella would go to the ball. The way was clear.

She let herself out of the house that evening very quietly and quickly before commonsense and cowardice forced her to change her mind. The air in the front garden had a foul chemical smell from the spray Arnold had put on the roses when he'd come home from the office.

She was glad when the warm, earthy scents of Mrs Loveday's garden enveloped her. Birds sang lustily, like an overture to the night's events. She could not think that they ever sang so sweetly on her side of the wall.

44

Cars were already parked in the lane. Mrs Loveday stood by the open door, splendid in a flowing black and gold dress. She pressed a glass into Mrs Paget's hand.

'A little concoction of my own, Nora, dear,' she cried. 'Come inside, do. I'm so glad you've come. You won't regret it.'

She was incredibly nervous as she saw enquiring faces turning towards her. Complete strangers. What would she find to say? She wasn't used to parties. She felt gauche, ill-equipped. She had been with Arnold too long. It would be a disaster. She quivered on the verge of fleeing.

'Have a sip of the punch, dear.' Mrs Loveday was at her side, eyes twinkling. 'That's it. Do you like it?'

'It's . . . it's delicious.' She took a larger sip, laughed apologetically. 'I don't drink much. Not at all, really. What is this?'

'Oh, wine, honey, spices, a dash of spirits . . . Not too sweet for you then?'

'Not at all.'

'Good. Then let me top up your glass. That's it. And come and meet a few people. Young Peter here. He's keen to conserve that field just by the woods. There's a developer been nosing around. But there are some rare orchids growing there . . . he'll be glad of your interest . . .'

She listened to Peter, was fascinated by his enthusiasm. Then she found herself giving her

45

own views while the punch fizzed in her head like shooting stars. She forgot about being sad and nervous. She forgot about the pathetic bundle of feathers on the compost heap, an image that had haunted her all day. She forgot about Arnold.

The room became crowded. Groups formed, dissolved, regrouped in other patterns. She moved with them. There was music and a space was cleared for dancing. She found herself dancing! And somehow it didn't matter that she'd never been to a dance in her life. She just followed the others, swaying and foot tapping to the rhythm. It was fun!

Peter struggled through the crush with a piece of paper. She signed the petition opposing any development on the orchid field. She felt bold and liberated.

'Every signature counts,' he said. 'Perhaps you'd like to come to our meetings sometime. We need caring people like you to protect our green spaces.'

She laughed. 'I might well do that.'

It was the alcohol of course. She was light-headed and it was a pleasant, freeing sensation. It allowed her to pretend that she had only herself to please and the devil take tomorrow.

Mrs Loveday cried, 'Food everybody.'

She went with the flow out onto the patio where lamps glowed softly as the sun went down and a barbecue sizzled. Someone heaped her plate and she wandered on into the garden where chairs had been set out and rugs flung onto the grass. The sky darkened to cobalt and lamps blossomed like yellow moons among the shrubbery.

The food melted exotically on her tongue. A young man drifted by bearing a pitcher of Mrs Loveday's punch.

'I've drunk far too much,' she protested as he refilled her glass. 'It's getting late. I should be going ...'

'No, no. Not yet,' he laughed. 'You can't possibly leave now. Why, you'd miss the best of the evening.'

But what if Arnold was home before she was? He would be incandescent with rage if he knew where she'd been. Her fingers trembled on the glass.

'We're almost ready to light the bonfire,' the young man said, lowering his voice and bending his head towards her as though it was some special secret he was sharing, 'and then, of course, there'll be music.'

'Will the flute player be here?' she asked. 'I've heard him ... from a distance, of course.'

'Ah, yes, you're new aren't you? To Mrs Loveday's parties?' His teeth glinted white as he smiled. He looked, she thought, like a young pagan with his strong brown throat and curly dark hair. She wished, fleetingly, that she were twenty again and free. He leaned closer, so that she felt his breath like a caress on her cheek. 'Yes, indeed, he'll be here. He'll play for us all. And especially for you, Nora Paget. A special song for you.'

With excited cries the bonfire was lit. Flames rushed and roared and sent spitting sparks into the velvety night air. People linked hands. Mrs Paget found herself caught up in a circle of dancers. Round and round the fire they pounded and she was laughing and breathless when she broke away. She stood under the pear tree, swaying a little from tiredness, from excitement. She felt as though ten years, twenty, had dropped away. Everyone had been so very kind. Not for one moment had she felt a wallflower. Always someone had been at her elbow to talk, to dance, to make her feel like one of the party.

A ripple of notes threaded through the laughter and chatter, faint at first then growing louder, stronger. Unexpected tears flooded her eyes as she was reminded of the nights she had lain in bed thinking of life passing her by. But the tears dried and she felt the music's pleasing resonance soothing and calming the niggle of worries in her head. It didn't matter about Arnold. She would cope with his anger. Nothing mattered but losing oneself in the music.

The dancers, as if at a signal, separated and sank to the trampled grass. Nobody spoke.

She found Mrs Loveday at her side, her strong warm fingers resting on her shoulder.

48

'Are you glad you came?' she whispered.

'Oh, yes. And the music. It's so very beautiful. Who is the player?'

'A friend. You shall meet him one day, but he is rather retiring and shy. He plays for our pleasure—for yours—but he prefers to remain out of sight.'

They listened for a moment and behind the music Mrs Paget heard a sound. A voice. Her breath caught in her throat.

'I think,' she whispered, 'I heard my husband call my name. He'll . . . he'll be wondering where I've got to. I should really go.'

'I heard nothing.' Mrs Loveday said.

The music was everywhere. It flowed through the black shadows of the garden, stirring the spitting embers of the bonfire where the three dogs sat like cut-outs silhouetted against the red glow.

Above Mrs Paget's head, on the wall, the two cats stared down intently into Arnold's garden. Despite Mrs Loveday's denials Mrs Paget could hear noises. Little thumps, rustlings, flutterings. The scrabble of tiny claws and wings. Shears clicking and clacking. But surely, she thought sleepily, Arnold wasn't out there working at this time of night.

Snick-snick-snick.

The clattering of branches and foliage full of life and spirit—yet there was no wind. And above all, the music growing louder, bolder,

49

filling her head with giddy spirals of sound.

I'm drunk, she thought, Quite stupidly drunk. I must go home.

As though she'd spoken aloud Mrs Loveday said softly, 'Stay a little longer. Then it will be the right time to leave.'

She wasn't sure how much later it was when she said her goodbyes. The music was dying now, fainter, slower, and as Mrs Loveday kissed her cheek she thought she caught a glimpse of the player of the pipes. It was a movement, merely, in the black shadowed shrubbery. A shaggy head turned towards her, a pair of odd shaped ears . . . She blinked and it might have been a clump of leaves.

She couldn't remember getting home. She awoke next morning, sprawled in unusual freedom across the double bed.

Her head didn't hurt, though the events of last night were filmy and blurred, as though viewed through a net curtain.

She said, 'Arnold?' and sat up. He wasn't in the bedroom.

She put on her dressing gown and slippers and went downstairs. The back door was open.

'Arnold,' she called. No answer. The garden seemed empty. She stared round. He was likely in the greenhouse. Then she saw that the shape of the birch tree was different. Oh, dear, it had lost a big branch. Perhaps Arnold was right and it did need cutting down.

She walked slowly down the path. Her

senses seemed particularly alert this morning. Scents, noises, sights seemed to be extra sharp.

Worm casts rose in tiny brown pyramids on the lawn which apparently had grown somewhat long overnight. The edges had a pleasing untidiness and snails had left silvery trails here and there.

She observed little things. A disorder among the pansies, rose petals lying carelessly on the gravel, a shrub that had sent out an enquiring twig to disturb the symmetry of its curved shape. The shears, heavily dewed, lay abandoned by the strawberry bed. They were tangled in netting that had been torn away and shredded. A blackbird cocked a round golden eye at her, its beak glistening with red juice. It didn't fly away as she passed.

Everything seemed endowed with vigorous life, even the tiny weed seedlings that were daring to poke up in the borders.

Something warm and furry curled round her legs. The marmalade cat smiled up at her as she scratched his chin. The black cat came scuttering across the lawn in pursuit of a tiny blue butterfly. It looked unafraid. Perfectly at home.

Arnold would have hurled something at it, flapped his arms, shouted.

But Arnold was over there under the tree branch, pinioned to the path, eyes wide and sightless. The branch had brought down a few panes of glass from the greenhouse. The

51

shards twinkled from various places on his body. His blood had seeped in tiny rivulets across the path and into the rich, dark, earth around the roots of the silver birch.

It came to Mrs Paget, entirely unbidden, that it was Midsummer's Day.

She stood there a moment, the sun fingering the brightness of her newly styled hair.

Then she heard Mrs Loveday call to her, and she smiled.

THE SHADOW QUEEN

'Mam's got a new baby.' The candle Clara held flickered its trembling, golden light across her round face. She looked solemn, older, as though the weight of the news had bestowed burdens, responsibilities. 'It's a little lad.'

Lizzie felt her mouth drop open.

'What she got that for?' she demanded, struggling to free herself from the demanding softness of the feather mattress and sit upright. 'Is Mam here? Has she come to take us home?'

'A message just come from Dad to Auntie Bea,' said Clara importantly. 'She said I could tell you straight off if you hadn't gone to sleep.'

'I was nearly. You woked me, our Clara,' The plaintive note in her sister's voice caused Clara to toss her head so that her heavy red plaits bounced against the frills of her pinafore.

'I'll get back downstairs then, seeing as you're not interested.' Clara flounced round so sharply that the candle flame streamed in a long horizontal streak and black shadows did a wild dance over the walls, giving momentary life to the stiff cabbage roses imprinted on the wallpaper.

'But I am interested. Honest,' Lizzie cried,

penitent. Even though the news was puzzling and unwelcome. How could Mam . . . after what happened to Peter . . . ?

She shivered. She didn't want to remember about Peter. Instead, she said pleadingly to her sister, 'Aren't you coming to bed?'

She felt lost in the big bed without Clara. And there were noises. Not the friendly noises she was used to. Clogs on cobbles and yowling cats and trains puffing and shunting in the junction yard. The country night was different. Full of strange cries and hootings and screechings. At home, when the wind got up and blustered round the houses, it gave her a warm, cosy feeling to be safe indoors. Here, the wind moaned and scratched at the windows like something, some THING, was about to break in and get her. And now there was this worse horror. Tom had told her today. Whispering in that sly, grinning way of his, the words slithering between his small brown teeth, telling her of the evil witch who lived right over her head in the cockloft and came out at midnight, looking for little girls to gobble up . . .

'It's not half past eight yet,' Clara said, but she relented. She wandered to the washstand and stood for a minute primping at her reflection in the glass. Auntie Bea had decreed that Clara, who was nearly ten, should have an extra hour downstairs if she sat quietly and helped with the mending. 'I always learned my

54

girls to be useful with the needle,' Auntie Bea had said, tut-tutting over Clara and Lizzie's lack of accomplishment. 'I don't know what our Mary-Ann can be thinking of. Not even showing you simple hemming. And in her circumstances an'all . . .' Words like 'daft' and 'feckless' hovered unspoken. 'Here, take this mutton cloth, Lizzie, and I'll show you . . .'

Lizzie, silently and rebelliously attacking the square of muslin that mangled itself under her clumsy fingers to something so grey and blood-spotted that she feared it would even be rejected for its intended use as a dishcloth, knew exactly what her mother, Mary-Ann, thought of when she sat, chin in hand, smiling dreamily over the warm, tumbled, dusty clutter of her kitchen. And it wasn't about dull things like polishing furniture and putting sheets side-to-middle and scouring the scullery flags, things around which Auntie Bea's day revolved. Mam had secrets, lovely golden secrets that she shared only with Lizzie. But she wasn't going to tell about that to Auntie Bea. Auntie Bea would sniff and look down her nose. And, worse, she might let on to Tom.

The thought of Tom knowing something like that about Mam, of twisting things in his vicious way made her go cold inside. She'd hated and feared him from that very first day, nearly two weeks ago, when he'd snatched her beautiful Ruby and dangled her over the water butt outside the scullery door. Ruby had real hair that Lizzie could put in rag curlers every night and proper clothes that you could put on and take off, even drawers with frills on and black shiny boots with tiny buttons.

'Shall us see if 'er can swim, then?' Tom had grinned.

'Don't!' Lizzie had cried, anguished. 'She'll drown!'

''Er's only a daft ol' doll.' He jerked his grubby fist down. Ruby's shiny black boots disappeared with a splash, the hem of her green skirt darkened as it soaked up the water.

Lizzie flew at him.

'Give her back!' She hammered with her fists on his stomach. 'Give her back or I'll tell on you!'

Tom's grin broadened. 'You do and you know what? Owd Johnson's bull'd be right after you. Tell-tale-tits allus gets chased by Johnson's bull.'

His words brought her up short. Johnson's bull was a fearsome creature. Lizzie and Clara had already walked down the lane to the farm for eggs and milk. Mrs Johnson had let them help to gather the warm eggs that the hens had laid only that morning and shown them the baby calves with the beautiful long-lashed eyes. And on the way they'd passed the dark, odorous barn where the monster was penned. It was hard to believe that this great brown beast had once been a gentle, timid calf. It swung its heavy head sullenly as it spied them over the half-door. It had little angry eyes and cruel curving horns sweeping up from tight packed curls on its head. It shifted restlessly, the brass ring shuddering in its nose as it snorted. Lizzie could feel how angry it was, how powerful and puffed up with wickedness. She had no need of Mrs Johnson's warning that they mustn't ever go near it.

So when Auntie Bea came crossly out of the scullery to see what Lizzie was making a fuss about and Tom casually tossed Ruby back at her and said, 'Oh, she nearly dropped her dolly in the butt. If I hadn't been here it'd have sunk right down,' she didn't say a word. She just hugged Ruby, damp and dripping, to her chest and hung her head while Auntie Bea scolded her for being such a nuisance.

'Does Tom know about our Mam and the baby?' she burst out now, to Clara's back, knowing before Clara spoke what the answer was. He was sitting downstairs, wasn't he? Having a game of cribbage or draughts with Uncle Sammy. He'd known before she, Lizzie, had. She felt betrayed.

And Clara was making it worse. ''Course, I knew about Mam getting the baby, ages ago,' she announced, full of self-importance.

'You didn't!'

'Did. That's why we're staying here.'

'You're fibbing me, our Clara. Mam would have told me an' all.'

'I'm big. You're only little.'

57

'I'm not little. I'm six.' Her voice quavered, then strengthened. 'You're telliing big fibs, our Clara. Auntie Bea only fetched us because Mam was poorly and needed a rest.'

Mam had lain in bed, white-faced and weary looking, her long hair, so like Clara's in colour but lank and dull now, spread untidily on the pillow.

'You'll be a brave girl, won't you love?' she'd said softly. 'It won't be for long and the country air will do you good.'

Lizzie had thrown her arms tightly round her mother's neck.

'But Mam, I don't want to go. I like it best here. Besides,' she'd added miserably, wanting to say so much and finding the words difficult for the tight ache in her chest and because Clara and Auntie Bea were hovering impatiently to make their own goodbyes, 'besides . . . you know—' her voice was a thread of breathy sound in Mam's ear, 'when we open . . . the secrets box . . .'

Her mother smiled and whispered so that only Lizzie could hear.

'It's easy, Lizzie love. Just shut your eyes and think very hard and the secrets box will be there, waiting for you to lift the lid. Your very own private, personal box, filled with all the lovely things you could ever want . . .'

But it hadn't been the same. She'd tried it. The pictures wouldn't come. She needed Mam to make her see the beautiful princesses, the castles, the magic landscapes, the adventures. Without Mam there wasn't anything.

She turned her thoughts reluctantly to the prospect of a new baby in the house. She supposed there was nothing she could do about it, but she was troubled all the same. And there was something she had to ask. Something important.

'Did she get the new baby from the same garden as our Peter?' Her voice came out loud and challenging.

Clara giggled. 'Garden? You're a right daft lump, you are. Babies don't come from gardens.'

'They do! Mam told me.'

Clara hesitated, a look that was both calculating and wary. Presently she said, 'What did Mam say—about this garden?'

'That there are lovely flowers there, like rainbows, and babies grow in 'em and live there until there's a nice Mam and Dad as want 'em. But Mam said our Peter was only loaned so he had to go back to be a rainbow flower.' Her bottom lip stuck out mulishly. Mam had said he was happier in the lovely, sunny garden. Lizzie had allowed herself to be comforted by the thought of him gurgling in the sunshine, rosy and plump-limbed, instead of thin and listless as he'd been when he lived with them. But it still hurt inside that he hadn't wanted to stay with her. She'd loved him so much. His special sister, Mam had said,

59

because he always stopped crying when she rocked his cradle by the fire and smiled his sweet toothless smile, his eyes following her round whenever she was in the room.

'You'll have to ask Mam about that when we get home,' Clara said carefully after a moment.

'But when are we going, Clara?'

'Dunno.' Clara shrugged and walked to the door. 'Week or two yet, I s'pose. Any road, I'm not bothered. It's nice here and Auntie Bea's going to learn me to crochet.' She held up the candle, grinning. 'Course it might snow or something—it gets right cold on t'moors, y'know—and we'd be trapped here all winter. No one'd be able to find us 'till they dug us out in spring.'

She closed the door, giggling, on Lizzie's wail of protest.

*   *   *

Lizzie pulled the sheet over her head and tried not to cry. It couldn't snow yet. The leaves were still on the trees and the hedges full of fat purple blackberries and red rosehips.

She wouldn't think about winter and snow. She wouldn't listen to the creaks and rustlings in the walls. She wouldn't think about the witch in the cockloft, waiting until the clock struck twelve when she would pounce out with long fangs and reaching claws.

Mam . . . Mam . . . why aren't you here? Where's the secrets box with all the lovely princesses and magic castles? I don't want to think about nasty, frightening things. An' why did you get another baby? We didn't want another after our Peter. I loved our Peter. I didn't want him to go away . . .

Everybody had been a baby once. It was hard to think about that. To imagine that Mam and Dad and Mrs Perkins-next-door who was so old that her face had shrivelled up all scribbly, and Auntie Bea and Uncle Sammy . . . people so big and clever . . . had once been small, helpless babies like their Peter. They must once have waited their turn for a Mam and Dad. Waited in the rainbow garden where the sun never stopped shining and the butterflies with soft powdery wings guarded them and birds sang for them and the air was full of lovely smells like when Mam baked bread or when you sniffed the yellow rosebush in the backyard after it had rained.

Even Tom must once have been a baby.

But he couldn't have come from the same place as our Peter. Tom was an orphan, any road. He didn't properly belong to Auntie Bea and he'd never had a Mam and Dad. It was only because he worked with Uncle Sammy at the mill down by the river and Auntie Bea had room now her girls were married and they'd took him in as a lodger. Orphans like Tom couldn't never have come from anywhere nice because a Mam and

Dad hadn't taken him in. The place where he'd come from could only be nasty. Black as night when the moon didn't shine and full of nettles and squirmy slimy slugs and bugs and soot and smelling like the gas works or the privy when it needed emptying...

A board creaked. She burrowed further under the sheet, hugging it so tightly about her head that the little pocket of air under the bedclothes grew stale and beads of sweat broke out on her face. Oh, why didn't Clara come to bed? The old witch in the cockloft was moving about already. Perhaps they'd forgotten the time downstairs. It must be long after half past eight. Nearly midnight.

The creak came again. She squeezed her eyes shut, gasping now, but not daring to raise the sheet an inch to let in fresh air in case ... in case the something she feared spied her through the gap and put its evil face close and hooked her out with a bony talon.

Mam. Mam, where are you?

She didn't want to think about the cockloft, but her thoughts crept like disobedient mice up and up. Through the ceiling, into the dusty, musty, beetly, spidery space under the slates.

Mam! The secrets box! I can't open the lid. I can't see the nice magic things. And the old witch'll get me any minute! I know it. Tom said...

And suddenly, blissfully, the picture was there behind her screwed up eyelids. Mam, laughing, reaching out with a gentle hand to touch her hair, to draw her onto her lap, as she always did.

'There, there, love. Nobody's going to hurt you. I'm here. And look, here's the box, just as it always was. Made of silver and gold and precious stones. Shall we open it and see if there's a story inside, waiting to be told? I'll just lift the lid—and look, Lizzie, look! There's the cockloft—no, don't be afraid—see, it's not like you thought it would be. There are fireflies and stars glowing everywhere like tiny lanterns. And can you see who's there in the corner, seated on a downy couch of angel's feathers? It's not a witch, is it? It's a princess— no, a queen! She's wearing a diamond crown and a dress woven from cobwebs and moonbeams and there are sapphires and emeralds braided into her long black hair. And d'you know what, Lizzie, love? She's come there specially all the way from a magic land far, far beyond the icy mountains of the North Pole just so as to watch over you and keep you safe as long as you're at your Auntie Bea's.'

'Oh, Mam,' she breathed. 'I can see her and she's smiling—an' she's beautiful and kind.'

'Course she is. Would I let anything ugly and horrible like a wicked old witch near my good little Lizzie? Now, remember, love, while I'm not with you, you must be brave,' Mam's's hold slackened. Lizzie could see that she was going sort've shimmery. She felt the touch

63

of her mother's lips against her hair. 'We'll be together again soon. Put your trust in the Shadow Queen. She'll not let harm come to you.'

'But the baby, Mam,' Lizzie cried. 'I wanted to ask you about it.'

'Joseph, that's what he's to be called,' Her mother's voice was faint as a whisper. 'You're the very first to know . . .'

The very first to know.

The words sang in Lizzie's head. She smiled as she slept.

*   *   *

She woke the next morning with the usual sinking feeling that Saturday brought.

At home she loved Saturday and Sunday. No horrible school when she might be picked out by Miss to spell a word or do a sum with the whole class watching. She could play hopscotch or bowl her wooden hoop in the street. Or perhaps Mam would take her into town ever so late to look for bargains in the market when all the lights were fizzing on the stalls and the prices were knocked down to get rid of stuff before the market packed up. And Mam said there was no need for anyone to go to chapel more than once on Sunday. They'd sometimes spend the whole afternoon in the park listening to the band. Or friends would come for tea and there'd be special things to eat like ham and seed cake.

It was different at Auntie Bea's. There was a lot of work to be done on Saturday. On Saturday everywhere had to be extra clean in readiness for Sunday. Lizzie was always given the ornately carved legs of the heavy table and chairs to polish before she was sent out with Clara to do the errands.

'And no skimping, mind, or you'll do them over again,' Auntie Bea said, in her sharp voice.

Sunday meant stiff clothes, chapel three times and listening to Uncle Sammy read stories from the Bible with long words she didn't understand. Her picture books were put away and she wasn't even allowed to take Ruby to chapel like she did at home. 'It's not seemly,' was Auntie Bea's final judgement as she rammed a hat pin into her black straw hat. 'And it's no use trying tears on with me, Lizzie. I'm not soft as duck muck like your Mam, so put your face straight and get on out.' She would feel the hard prod of Auntie Bea's fingers between her shoulder blades, but that didn't hurt nearly as much as leaving poor Ruby all alone and pining in her best frock when Lizzie knew Ruby wanted to go out.

But worse than all these things was the fact that Tom was at home. At dinner time on Saturday he and Uncle Sammy came up the valley road from the mill. He'd be grinning or whistling and as soon as he saw Lizzie he'd shout, 'Watch out little 'un. Tom's back. I've got me eye on you, so don't you get up to no mischief.' And though Uncle Sammy would laugh and ruffle her hair as though what Tom said was no more than a joke, Lizzie felt fear shiver up her spine. Tom's grin never reached his eyes. She knew his jolly words really meant, *Watch out, I'm going to get you. And when I do it'll be the worse for you, little brat.*

Though she did her best to keep out of his way at weekends, he was right crafty. He knew just when to sneak up on her and wrench off the big white bow that fastened her plait and throw it into the brambles, so that she got herself all scratched finding it and a telling-off from Auntie Bea into the bargain for losing it in the first place. He knew exactly how and where to pinch her arms and legs with his big rough fingers so that it hurt most and showed least. And he knew how much it terrified and pained her when he tortured her lovely Ruby. Rudely lifting her skirts to show her drawers, pulling her hair so hard that some of the fine yellow strands came out of the china scalp, snatching her from Lizzie's arms and whirling her round by her foot until her boot came off and she pitched into the muddy ground.

Lizzie knew better than to run to Auntie Bea. 'Can't do wi' mardy babies,' was all the sympathy she got. 'Learn to take a bit of teasin' or you'll grow up wi'out any backbone. Now get from under me feet . . .'

This morning Lizzie lay in bed and tried to recall the warm, comforting feeling she'd had last night when Mam had talked to her. *Put your trust in the Shadow Queen.* Last night she'd been so certain, so relieved, that it wasn't a witch in the cockloft but a beautiful and kind lady who would watch over her. Last night she hadn't been afraid at all. Now, she stared up at the whitewashed ceiling and felt the tendrils of fear creeping back like a clinging, unpleasant mist. Tom was as real and big and solid as Johnson's bull. She could reach out and touch the both of them if she dared. They could certainly touch her, harm her. The Shadow Queen might be as brave and beautiful as Mam said, but she wasn't solid. She was far off, like the secrets box. It was difficult to imagine the storyworlds of the secrets box when Mam wasn't there. Perhaps the Shadow Queen's magic only worked after dark when Mam was talking, whispering, holding her safe.

All her certainties fled as the morning wore on. Clara was full of herself which made everything worse. Auntie Bea was letting her help with the baking. She beat butter and sugar with a wooden spoon in a bowl, her face almost as red as her hair. 'Have you done the dusting properly' she asked in the same sharp tone as Auntie Bea, when Lizzie wandered into the kitchen.

'It's not fair,' Lizzie said sulkily, 'me having to do your dusting as well as me own.'

'Nowt in this life's fair,' snapped Auntie Bea, straightening up from the oven with a great brown crusted pie in her tea cloth-covered hands. She laid it on the table and stared at it in satisfaction. A smell of savoury steam filled the kitchen. 'Sooner you learn that, Lizzie, the better. Now while Clara finishes the pudding you can go down to Johnson's for a dozen eggs.'

'By meself?'

'It's nowt but a cock stride.' She lifted a basket down from its hook on a black beam. "Sides you can look out for your Uncle and Tom and tell'em to get a move on or their dinner'll be spoilt. And you'll need two hands, so don't go taking that doll.'

Lizzie took the basket. If it hadn't been a Saturday she'd have felt important going to the farm by herself. Not that she had any intention of going alone. Away from Auntie Bea's eagle eye she snatched up Ruby from where she'd been sitting on the step taking the air because of the Bad Head she'd woke with and hid her in the basket. Perhaps if she was very quick she'd be there and back before she saw Tom.

She ran into the lane. She could see almost all its empty length from here. It wriggled like a dusty grey worm down the hill, between the drystone walls that marked Farmer Johnson's fields, past the farmhouse, then down to the village, across the river by a humpy bridge and on to the big square block of the mill.

68

She ran as fast as she could down towards the farmhouse. As she turned the last corner she saw Tom trudging towards her.

Alone. Oh, no! Uncle Sammy must've stopped as he sometimes did for a glass of stout at the Red Lion and there was Tom, an evil grin splitting his face when he saw her. He began to run.

She stopped dead, then in a mad panic flew for the wall and climbed over it into the field. The grass was tussocky. She stumbled so that Ruby nearly fell out of the basket. It wasn't far. She only had to get down the field, through the open gate and she was in the farmyard. She'd be safe there. Mrs Johnson would be sure to be about or Farmer Johnson or one of his men.

'Eh you! Come 'ere!' Tom was thudding after her. He had long strong legs that could eat up the ground. She could almost feel his breath on the back of her neck, his hands reaching out for her . . .

Mam! Mam she screamed in her head. *He's going to get me.*

Remember what I told you . . . The Shadow Queen will keep you safe.

And, suddenly, there she was! The Shadow Queen. Drifting across the grass, like a stray pearly moonbeam in the mellow autumn sunlight. Fragile, indistinct as a wisp of mist, her jeweled garments billowing and fading, her long hair streaming behind her like black watery silk.

. . . *Don't be afraid, Lizzie. He won't hurt you.* Her voice was comfortable, gentle, a bit like Mam's. Lizzie felt a cool incandescence drift around her. It was like being masked in dappled shade when the day was too hot. The thought sprang into her head. I mustn't run. People like Tom have to be faced up to. She stopped so suddenly that Tom almost cannoned into her.

'You daft beggar!' he yelled, his boots slithering as they fought for purchase on the damp grass.

'Stop following me,' she said, her voice sounding thin and pitifully squeaky, even though she was trying to be brave.

The field stretched round them. Empty. Useless. She thought she could hear voices, shouts. Down in the yard, perhaps. Farmer Johnson's men. Too far away to save her.

Tom thrust his face down to hers. His eyes were piggy little slits. He bared his teeth. 'Ah'll follow you if I feel like it. An' I'll do this if I feel like it.' He caught the soft flesh of her cheek between his rough nails and squeezed tightly. 'And this.' He released her and made a grab at Ruby hanging perilously over the basket's edge. She swung the basket away, her cheek stinging so that tears came to her eyes.

'Aye, I'll mek you cry,' he sneered. 'Nobody to run to 'ere, is there? Nobody to see.'

'There is!' she cried. 'There is. Right here.

70

An' . . . An' she'll punish you. 'Cos she's magic.'

He chuckled evilly. 'Magic, eh? Come on then. Show me.'

She stood very still, staring past him. She felt suddenly very peaceful, very secure. It was happening. The Shadow Queen was going to rescue her. It was like Mam said. She'd had no need to be afraid.

'What yer staring at? What's that racket?' Tom's head swiveled round. She'd thought of the worst thing that could happen to Tom. Now it was about to happen and she would watch and be glad because of all the nasty things he'd done to her and to Ruby.

'Oh, help . . .' Tom looked about wildly.

'It's a punishment,' she said, calmly taking Ruby out of the basket and settling her in the crook of her arm so that she could watch too. 'You're to be punished. That's the magic.'

'T'bull's out!' Tom screamed. 'And t'gate's open . . . it's coming this way!'

'It's coming for you,' Lizzie said. 'Me an' Ruby's all right.'

The bull paused in the gateway, head down, pawing the ground with its hoof. Behind it men, puny little figures against its angry bulk, ran with ropes and sticks. They waved their arms, shouting to Tom and Lizzie, 'Get out o' the way! Get over t'wall.'

Lizzie stood. No need for her to go. Tom began to run, mindless of her, thinking only

71

of his own skin. The bull roared, spying the running figure with its evil, bloodshot eye and began to lumber forward.

Tom tripped and fell. His scream seemed to echo up and up towards the clouds, back and forth from the green flanks of the moors. He floundered helpless on the tussocky grass.

This is what you want, Lizzie? Mam's voice, the Shadow Queen's voice. She wasn't sure which. *There'll be no rainbow garden for him, remember.*

'I know,' she said. 'Just a nasty black stinky place. Which he deserves.'

Well?

The bull was gathering speed, thundering up the field towards the shrieking, flapping object on the ground. The thing that it instantly hated with all its angry, frustrated heart.

The question hovered. Lizzie felt the power of it surging in her veins. She had an odd feeling of detachment. Of standing apart watching herself, the bull, the frightened boy on the grass, as though all three were frozen, unmoving, waiting for her to give the answer. The right answer.

And flowing between them, the shimmering form that curled and wreathed and flowed like moonlit water.

Lizzie sighed. 'I don't want him really to be hurt,' she said. 'I don't like anyone being hurt. But he didn't care about hurting me. Or Ruby.'

He knows no better. Perhaps no one has ever

72

shown him how to be kind, how to love. Will you give him the chance to learn?

Lizzie considered the boy spreadeagled helplessly on the grass. Not such a big lad, after all. Skinny really, his feet swamped by over-large boots, his legs like thin sticks below his rough cord breeches. Or perhaps in some funny way she herself had grown in the last few moments so that they were more evenly matched in size.

She sighed again. And answered.

*   *   *

Afterwards it was reckoned a miracle. The way the lad leapt to his feet and hurled himself over the wall in the nick of time. The way the bull had slowed to a halt, staring around in a bewildered sort of way until they'd managed to get ropes on him and lead him back to the barn, gentle as a lamb now he'd worked off his bad temper. The way that little lass had stayed so brave and still.

Only Lizzie knew.

She'd watched, fascinated, as the ethereal, shadowy drift of jeweled mist swept across to Tom. She saw how the slim, pale arms had raised him as though he weighed feathers rather than flesh and bone. And, so swiftly and easily, he'd been lifted over the wall away from danger.

Once the bull was caught, she went across

73

and climbed onto the wall. She lifted Ruby to see Tom cowering below, his face the colour of ash, tears of fright and relief squeezing between his pale, stubby lashes.

'See, Ruby,' she said, smiling. 'Nothing to be afraid of, is there? He's crying just like the new baby that's come to live at our house. You didn't know he was going to be called Joseph, did you Tom?'

He's only a poor orphan. She thought. Nobody really loves him. Not even Auntie Bea and Uncle Sammy. They only give him house room because they feel sorry for him and there's no one else to care.

Tom blinked up at her. He looked as bewildered as the bull.

'What you on about?' he said sullenly, knuckling his eyes with a grubby fist and scrambling unsteadily to his feet. But the fire, the threat had gone from him.

She continued to smile at him. She wasn't going to explain now. There'd be time in the next week or two. Plenty of time.

Tom turned away, as though her smile somehow defeated him. He began to walk up the lane, limping, shoulders bowed against the weight of her victory.

It wasn't right, Lizzie thought sadly, that someone should be as lonely as all that. And she didn't really need what he needed . . . She was strong enough now, loved and with love to spare.

She stood there lost in thought, her lips moving silently as though she spoke to herself. And presently, drifting away from her up the lane she saw the jeweled mist that flowed round the indistinct, shimmering figure of a woman. It hung for a moment in Tom's wake, then in a tender, gentle movement, it wrapped itself protectively around his thin frame.

Tom hesitated, lifting his head, staring round in surprise as though he heard someone call his name. Then he shrugged, squared his shoulders and walked on with a lighter step, while Lizzie skipped away down the field, hugging Ruby to her heart.

HANTU-HANTU

I put on my shoe and scream. Nurse Kelly, the nice red-headed one, Karen, takes off my shoe and holds it up and says, 'Look, nothing at all, Jane. Nothing. You imagined it.' And the new sneery nurse, the man, says, 'You shouldn't pander to her. She only wants attention. She'll have to learn to stand on her own two feet when she's out in the community.'

There's a joke in there somewhere. Shoes. Feet. I don't laugh. I cling to Karen's hand. I'd felt it squirming between my toes. Ready to scuttle up my leg, hide in my clothes, rattle over my body with its hard fast little feet . . .

Karen's a lovely girl. She takes me into breakfast because she can see how trembly I am. She talks about her boyfriend and the rock concert they're going to on Saturday. I'm composed by the time she leaves me. I can face up to searching my cereal. Making sure. Their eggs are the worst, you see. Little brown shiny packets. Easy to mistake for malted wheat husks. Karen says they're very particular in the kitchens and if everything's piping hot I don't worry too much. If they're cooked, they're dead, aren't they? On the other hand they can lay eggs in anything, anywhere. That's why they're so successful.

Karen reminds me a lot of Susan. Bubbly,

red-headed. I like Karen but when she's not on duty I try not to think of her too much because I only start to remember Su. I've been such a lot better lately, I've kept Su right away. But with the damned thing in my shoe this morning the pictures won't go.

I didn't want them to change my tablets. I told Karen. She said the doctors know best and there's this new drug.

There's always a new drug. Some of them work, some don't.

Su had red hair and freckles just like Karen. It was quite the wrong colouring for someone living in the tropics. She never tanned properly, but she didn't need a tan. All those young servicemen, married or not they honed in on Su like wasps drawn to a ripe August fruit. She could pick and choose and she did, but nothing heavy, nothing serious. I marvelled at her. She played the field without worry or conscience. I couldn't do that. I was shy of men, too inhibited. I was an only child born to worried, middle-aged parents who built invisible fences round their dull lives, trapping me in with them. The sound of apron strings snapping was still loud in my ears. I never woke to a new day in that new country without a sense of amazement and guilt that I'd made the break, defying my mother's tears, my father's accusations of disloyalty which were no less pointed for being silent; stares and sighs and head-shakings, laden with reproach and regret at my selfishness in putting half the world between us.

Su and I travelled out on the same plane. Propellers, then, of course. Three days with overnight stops in New Delhi and Calcutta. The shock of India. The squalor, the poverty, the smells. We were a bit fearful of what we'd find in Singapore after that. But Singapore was lush and green and sleepily colonial. We were still top of the heap then, in the fifties, Europeans, Brits. Ex-pats with an in-built sense of superiority and foreign service allowances that enabled us to live in a style to which we rapidly became accustomed.

Su and I shared a flat in Tanglin. The school where we taught catered for children of servicemen and we were civilians signed up for a three-year tour of duty.

The flat had cool terrazzo floors and a shady balcony where we sat in the evenings drinking ice-cold Tiger beer. We had a Chinese *amah* who lived in a cubbyhole in the back and kept house for us. We learned to drive and bought second-hand cars and new cameras so we could take photographs of ourselves in shorts or sundresses to dazzle the folks back home. We bought hand-embroidered linen for next to nothing at C.K.Tang's in River Valley Road and went to Raffles for Sunday curry tiffin.

We acclimatised to the soporific steamy heat, easily able in our busy lives to blot out the unpleasant bits. The stink of the polluted river mouth so photogenic with its clutter of sampans and tokangs and its sweating, ragged coolies. The poverty and disease and violence that simmered in the picturesque *kampong*s and behind the scabrous, bustling overcrowded alleyways of Chinatown.

And the wildlife.

Everybody had a snake story to tell. The krait found slithering towards the baby's cot, the python in the monsoon drain. Or *a chikchak* story. The one that dropped from the ceiling into the lady's cleavage, the one that landed in the soup at a posh dinner party. I never saw a snake and I liked the little lizards. After all, they were useful, eating up the moths and mosquitoes. It was the insect life that worried me.

Mosquitoes. 'Give it a year and they won't bother you so much,' the old hands said. 'They like freshly-arrived blood.' The praying mantises with their swivelling, bulbous heads, the six-inch centipedes with the vicious bites and the small shiny brown millipedes that curled up tight at a touch, the ants that poured into the flat in brown or black streams in search of food. The giant cockroaches that flew in at night and lived in the drains, the kitchen cupboards, the wardrobes. Everywhere.

I disliked the cockroaches most of all.

Just dislike at first. Because they were destructive and filthy and a nuisance. The hate, the terror came later.

Su laughed at me. 'Queen of the Flit spray,' she called me. I never went anywhere without the big tin spray. No handy aerosols in those days. I never slept in any room unless it had been drenched in insecticide. I burned green coils that gave off fumes supposed to keep the night air free of mosquitoes. I slept under a mosquito net long after Su had given up. I poured boiling water and undiluted Jeyes fluid down every grid and lined the kitchen shelves with specially impregnated paper.

I still got bitten. The ants still found their way into the sugar. The cockroaches kept on coming.

But, in the end, my caution—my precautions—saved me. Though there have been times, screaming, blood-red times, when I wished I hadn't bothered.

Sometimes I think Su was the lucky one. And that's the sickest of black jokes.

*   *   *

'The sun's nice today,' Karen says. 'Why don't you take your knitting outside?'

She's trying to catch me out. I laugh to let her know I know. She grins back.

'I might,' I say. 'When I've finished this decreasing.'

The dayroom does get stuffy. Too much glass. Added on to the gaunt Victorian

80

building in the sixties and never satisfactory. Built cheaply and it shows. Draughty in winter, too hot in summer. No matter, it'll all be pulled down soon. The place is half empty already. Been sold to a property developer, I understand, for houses and shops.

I don't want to leave here, where I've learned to feel safe. But they don't listen to me. They don't understand about the danger. They just smile and tell me I'll soon settle in the nice new house with nice new friends and nice kind people to look after us. Nice. Everything's going to be nice. Perhaps it seems like it for them.

I finish my few rows and wrap up the knitting in a towel, then in the usual three plastic bags and when Karen has her back turned I take the aerosol out of my handbag and quickly spray the outside of the parcel. She doesn't like to see me doing that. Goes on about the ozone layer. I put the parcel on the table in the sun. It'll be safe in the sun. They don't like the sun. I wouldn't ever take my knitting into the garden. You never know what might get tangled up in it.

'I'm going out now,' I say, replacing the aerosol in my bag. 'Just for a breath of air.'

Karen looks from the parcel to me and shakes her head in an exasperated sort of way. I pretend not to notice and march out briskly to show that I don't care.

81

*   *   *

It was Su's idea to go away for a few days that first Easter.

'Harry's getting to be a pain in the neck,' she said. Harry was the latest besotted admirer, pursuing Su with the same determination that had won him his wings. 'Every time a Hurricane flies over I think it's him keeping an eye on me. Let's take the Pontianak and flee up country, eh?'

Up country was Malaya, not Malaysia, then. Attached to Singapore by the fragile thread of the man-made causeway. We'd been no further than Johor Bahru and come the long summer holidays we'd go up to Kuala Lumpur and to Fraser's Hill in the cool mountains. The Emergency was almost over, the Communist guerillas being driven further and further north. Curfews being lifted everywhere. Whole areas being declared 'white'.

The west coast, on an impulse, at Easter? Why not?

Sue's car was an American Pontiac. A big saggy monster with rusting edges. She'd nicknamed it after we heard the Malay legend of the Ponianak, a vampire who terrorised women after childbirth, scooting about the jungle trailing her innards and wearing her breasts on the back.

It was a joke to us, of course

Vampires. Ghosts, *hantu-hantu.* We giggled

82

over reports in the local papers. Phantoms terrorising travelers on a particular stretch of road, hauntings in a rubber plantation, an old house . . . Ghosts were taken very seriously by the Malays and Chinese. But we were sensible Brits, weren't we?

We laughed at such superstitious nonsense and Su cheerfully called her car Pontianak. After all, we were not of this steamy, red-earthed land. Its devils were not ours. We were from harder, colder latitudes and if there was any apprehension about our journey, it was of comprehensible things like terrorists or even tigers that were known, occasionally, to spring out from the jungle onto an unsuspecting passer-by.

The roads ran through long dark avenues of rubber trees, through tiny stilt-housed *kampongs* where children and chickens scratched in the pink dust under banana trees and coconut palms, through swatches of jungly forest, the trees grown tall and skinny in their greed for light and air, swathed in ropes and curtains of twining, strangling creeper. The ones that grew too tall, too old, too heavily burdened, crashed defeated down to the seething, crawling, wriggling life in the soft wet decay of the forest floors.

Living jungle is always full of dead things. Something dies. Something else eats it in order to exist. But we didn't think about that. We saw only the beauty of it because that was what we wanted to see. The butterflies with wings of black velvet and yellow and shot blue satin fluttering at the forest edge. A red and turquoise kingfisher regarding us from a telegraph pole. Blinding white thunderheads rising into the arch of the sky above the dense dark green mounds of forest.

Snap. Snap. Snap. The camera clicked. The images frozen into black and white stiffness. Recorded to be sent dutifully home in the next letter, the letter never to be written.

*   *   *

I walk quickly between the neat lawns and flowerbeds. I walk in the exact middle of the path, my sturdy shoes going click-clack on the concrete, swivelling my head from side to side, ever watchful. Near the buildings it's okay. Lots of space. Nowhere for them to hide. Where the paths converge near the main gate overgrown shrubs—laurel mostly—intrude onto the concrete making a dark tunnel. They should be cut down. I've told them. But nobody bothers. I pull my skirts tightly round my knees and rush through. When I'm safely on the wide main drive I look back at the masses of dark glossy leaves shining like enamel in the sun, at the leggy ending stalks rising from an innocent litter of discarded plastic bags and drink cans.

Nothing here. Not in daylight. Not in

sunlight. I wouldn't come out here at dusk, of course. Never. I know the risks.

I've been safe here for nearly thirty years. Protected by my caution, my alertness, my fear. I am surrounded, guarded, by people who have sympathy with my fear and believe in my madness.

I was mad once, of course. Properly mad. My brain convulsed to jangling chaos. The violence of my terror turning me into another self entirely. But I am long years now from the padded cell, the locked ward, though I feel the heavy shadow of that other self as I stand on the drive and stare through the open gates to the traffic that passes on the road.

I have become, my guardians explain kindly, an institutionalised victim of out-of-date medical practices. I should have been returned to the real world years ago. I will be so much better when I have learned to enjoy the freedom of a new life.

They are so knowledgeable and clever. And such fools.

*　　　*　　　*

We stayed at the Rest House, a long, low building with a red tiled roof and deep verandahs drenched in purple and pink bougainvillea. Across the road was a beach of yellow sand fringed with leaning palm trees. We swam each morning before breakfast in the warm, cloudy waters of the Indian Ocean and again in the late afternoon when we came in hot and sticky from sightseeing.

'Don't you ever sit down and relax?' DP enquired one evening from the depths of his rattan chair as we ran indoors, trailing sand from our flip-flops, one evening.

'Why should we?' Su called cheerfully.

'Lemme buy you a drink,' he said. 'And you can tell me what I'm missing.'

'Thanks, but no thanks,' Su said, whisking past him.

Su had christened him DP, for Drunken Planter, and dismissed him as a bore. He was a small, pale, damp young man with restless eyes, his hand permanently wrapped round a half-filled glass. Whenever we were indoors he always seemed to be there beside us. Drifting from a shady corner to offer us a drink, passing our bedroom door as we opened it, leaning across from the next table at breakfast to interrupt our conversation with some anecdote of his own.

Only that morning Su's patience had run out. 'Do you mind? This is a private conversation,' she'd snapped at breakfast, when he sniggered at something she'd said to me.

Heads turned at other tables. DP smiled his bland, absent smile and turned his attention back to his toast. He was uncowable. Perhaps it was the permanent fix of alcohol in his veins

86

that insulated him from insult. From reality. From everything, poor lost soul.

An hour later he was swaying over me, breathing whisky fumes down my neck as I sat on the verandah writing postcards while Su was indoors washing her hair.

'Pretty girl, your friend,' he said. 'Su, isn't it? Got spirit. I like that . . .'

I leaned away from him and pretended to write, but I wasn't Su. Good manners had been instilled in me from childhood. Smile, be polite, respond to small talk. I couldn't be rude to him, make a scene.

We held a stilted conversation. Mostly he asked the questions, but he volunteered one or two snippets of his own. His name was Charles Smith. The rubber estate he managed had turned him into a bit of a hermit, really, because it was the most beautiful spot on earth and he hated to leave it. He struggled to bring a photograph out of his pocket. 'Here,' he said. 'That's me in the garden, with my friends.'

But my reaction was rather more positive than he'd reckoned with. As I glanced at the snap, I saw, out of the corner of my eye, a slither of movement between the wooden planks of the verandah near my feet. I squealed, dropping the photograph and leaping up and away.

'A cockroach! There! There!' He looked bewildered, bending slowly and squinting into the crack.

'It's coming out! Stamp on it!'

He blinked, bemused. He reached down. 'This?' he said. 'This? You're not scared of a poor old cocky, are you?'

He slid it over and over in his hands, the cockroach running, dancing, sliding in and out of his fingers.

'How could you?' I said, shuddering, unable to watch.

'Fancy being scared,' he said. 'I bet your friend Su isn't scared.' He moved suddenly, pushing his hands with the brown shiny creature rushing madly over them, towards me. 'Here. Look. It's harmless.' His voice sounded different. He was enjoying himself.

'Don't!' I cried, cringing back. 'Don't!'

'Okay, okay,' he said. 'Look. It's gone now.'

'Where?' I looked at his empty hands.

'Threw it into the garden.'

'You should have killed it!' My voice trembled.

'Everything has its place in nature,' he said. 'Even the humble cockroach.' His voice was flat again now. Bland. His hand reached out and touched my bare arm. I flinched.

'I have to go,' I snatched up my postcards and fled.

The pads of his fingers and thumb seemed to have left separate damp, cold indentations in my skin. I found myself rubbing at them absently at odd times through the day. I didn't say anything to Su about what had happened. I

88

was secretly ashamed of myself for being such a scaredy cat over the cockroach. Besides, Su might have said something to him. Been sharp. Made a scene.

*   *   *

I scuff the lining of my coat against my arm. The five separate numb areas respond with a faint, cold tingle. I've grown used to them, fond of them, almost. They remind me to be on my guard. Doctors have examined my arm. I've had tests, scans. They say there's nothing the matter, they think it's all in my head. They would, of course. They're the sane ones. I'm the madwoman.

The wind sweeps up the drive stirring the dust and the litter. Clouds are building over the council estate opposite the hospital grounds. It'll rain later. The day was too bright, too soon.

Cars swish past the gate. It's a busy road. They'll take me out along that road when it's time, in the blue hospital minibus. Past the park, past the shops, through the streets of neat suburban houses to my new home. Out in the community, where I'll be so much better.

That's what they say. That's what they believe.

I'd like to believe it, too.

*   *   *

89

Later, we went poking around the ruins of the old Portuguese fort above the town. It wasn't a tourist asset then. There weren't any tourists. The walls sheltered heaps of tumbled, overgrown stone blocks. A crumbling statue of St Francis Xavier stared forlornly out to sea, features blurred by years of exposure to tropical rain and relentless sun. The noon shadows were black in the angles of the grey, mossy walls.

'Look who's there,' Su said, tugging me behind a bolster of creeper swathing a buttress. 'Our drunken acquaintance, no less.' Then she paused and whistled softly. 'But take a gander at his chums.'

I peered round her shoulder, screwing up my eyes against the dazzle.

They stood in one of the deep black patches of shadow. For a moment I had the illusion of dark bulky shapes, appearing to press themselves tightly against the wall as though shrinking back from the hard white sun. But it was a trick of the light. As my eyes adjusted I saw there were three people standing deep in conversation, heads bent, absorbed. Charles Smith in his crumpled white cotton trousers and open-necked shirt. The other two . . .

'Aren't they . . . isn't he *something*?' Su breathed.

Something.

What exactly? Malay? Chinese? Indian?

Some exotic Eurasian blend.

Something. Golden people.

The brown and ivory batiks they wore seemed to shimmer and flow in the shadow. The woman wore topaz-petalled orchids in her oiled hair. The man's sleek, dark head seemed part of the shadow itself, his thin, beautiful profile seemed etched upon it.

As though he sensed watchers, he turned his head.

I dodged back. Su did not move. I yanked at her arm.

'Come on. Let's go.'

'In a minute,' she said, 'I must see . . .'

She continued to stare round the creeper. Silent. Very still. I could hear the soft sigh of her breathing in the silence, see the flush that the sun had raised on her thick, pale, lightly freckled skin.

'Come *on,*' I said. We were in the full sun. Sweat was prickling down my back. 'If DP sees us he'll only tag on. We don't want him following us around all afternoon.'

'What?' she said, vaguely.

'DP,' I repeated. 'Oh, don't just stand there.'

I pulled her back roughly. For a moment she staggered off balance. She looked dazed, distant.

'Sorry,' I said. 'We must hurry.'

I don't think she heard me, but she followed me meekly enough down the track through the long grasses to where the Pontianak waited to take us on to fresh pleasures.

*   *   *

The wind nips my ears and my ungloved fingers. I hunch my shoulders against it and continue my walk, suddenly wanting to be back in the dayroom with its familiar stuffy smell. Needing the security of its cracked walls and smeary windows.

I don't want to be here looking beyond the gates into the blind abyss of the future.

I don't want to think of Su.

I hate the pictures in my head. Like the television in the dayroom. Always on even if nobody's watching. But the pictures in my head are compulsory viewing. Can't shut my eyes and have forty winks or get on with my knitting or enjoy my walk. The new tablets. Not working. I'll tell them when I get back. Tell Karen.

No help to me now, though.

I walk so fast I'm almost running, but I can't escape the technicolour newsreel in my head.

*   *   *

We went back early to the Rest House. Su seemed unaccustomedly listless.

'Bit of a headache,' she confessed. 'Probably the sun. I'll take a couple of aspirin and lie

92

down for an hour.'

I went for a swim, but I didn't stay on the beach long. It wasn't the same without her. I felt conspicuous on the acres of empty sand, imagining the passers-by on the road above exchanging rude comments about my large, awkward shape. Thinking that the small Malay boys from the *kampong* near the beach, tumbling like sleek puppies in the waves, saw me as an intruder.

I expected to find Su napping, but the curtains weren't even drawn in our room. Her bed was pristinely empty. When I'd showered and changed I discovered her in the bar, curled up in one of the shabby rattan chairs. The glass-topped table between her and Charles Smith held half-filled beer mugs. He saw me first, rose politely to his feet, his bland smile broadening.

'What'll it be? Beer? Gin and tonic?'

'Oh, I don't think . . .' I began, nervously wondering whether Su really was sickening for something to have allowed herself to be cornered by this person she so despised. 'Are you all right, love? Your headache . . .'

Su's glance slid from mine, but not before I'd seen the flash of exasperation, of impatience.

'Do sit down if you're stopping,' she said, pettishly. 'I'm fine now.'

I felt hurt and surprised. I sat down, not knowing what else to do. The other two

93

ignored me. Su was talking to Charles Smith as though he were some new acquaintance she wanted to impress. As though, in my absence, they had together crossed some watershed of understanding and I was a straggler left miles behind, struggling to catch up.

'I don't know what got into you,' I said, still peeved, as we walked in the warm velvety evening darkness towards the hissing pressure lamps and crowded stalls of the *amah's* market laid out under the palm trees.

'It's not *him*, you clot,' Su said lightly, but with a touch of that same hurtful impatience. 'It's the other one. His friend.'

'Friend?' I said in bewilderment.

'The one we saw up at the fort.' She laughed. 'He's the one I'm interested in.'

I gawped at her but she wasn't looking at me. She was looking at a display of garish plastic sandals laid out under a tree. Not seeing them, either. Her smile was distant, dreaming.

'He—they—Charles' friends, they're sister and brother. And royalty, no less. "An ancient lineage" to quote Charles. Oh, some minor offshoot I've no doubt. Wrong side of the blanket for all I know. Very ally-pally with our DP, though. Live near to him in some jungly *istana* out in the *ulu*. It sounds—well—silly to say this, but something happened when I looked at him. Eyes across a crowded room and all that jazz.'

'You mean, that man . . . and you . . .'

'I never believed it could happen. Instant attraction. An instant of knowing, absolutely, that he felt the same.' She shrugged. 'Fate. Kismet. Call it what you like. Pazaam. It happened right there in the fort. That's all I can tell you.' The lightness of her tone belied the trusting, defenceless, almost pleading expression in her eyes.

I was moved by her confession. It was so silly and romantic and so unlike her that it must be true. And who was I, whose experience with men, with love, was limited by the inhibitions of my upbringing, to deny that she was right?

'You may not believe me,' she said, 'but try to understand.'

I did try, but when she added, almost offhandedly, that Charles Smith had asked us to stay at his place for a day or two on the way back to Singapore, I couldn't stop myself. 'Good heavens, we can't do that! We don't know anything about him!'

'We're past the age of white slave traders,' Su snapped. 'Grow up. He's a perfectly respectable bloke. We're together, what could possibly—' She broke off, her glance sliding past me. 'Look,' she breathed on a small, trembling, satisfied sigh, 'look, they're there . . .'

I shaded my eyes against the flare of the pressure lamps. They stood beneath the tufted

95

palms, the light catching the curve of an arm, the glint of a jewel. Charles Smith waved. The figures either side of him stood in a kind of proud, watchful stillness. Royalty, Su had said, but despite my scepticism, it seemed that regal was the only adjective that fitted.

The man's head was turned, his gaze locked upon Su.

I looked from one to the other. Reluctantly becoming aware that whatever it was between them—this unspoken emotion, this sexual, animal compulsion—it was almost palpable on the heavy night air. Like the cloying, clinging waft of perfume from a flower-laden frangipani. The tree invisible, its presence overpowering.

I felt suddenly alone and excluded.

I caught the woman's eye. His sister. I wondered if she too felt the same sense of exclusion, of shock. He was her brother, after all. And it was odd but it seemed that her head dipped in acknowledgement and her shoulders lifted delicately, as though she, too, sensed my thoughts and rued what was happening.

Accept it, a soft voice in my head murmured. *Bend with the wind. It will blow over like a sudden storm. No harm done. You and I, we will guard this foolish, hot headed pair until they come to their senses. Until then, be easy, my friend. Trust me.*

I blinked in surprise, Had I actually heard her voice above the racket of the market? I

96

stared at her, saw the gleam of her eyes, the whiteness of her gentle smile. I found myself smiling back, feeling an unexpected rush of warm kinship with her. Of course I could trust her. How lucky I was to have the opportunity of meeting such a charming and interesting woman. A royal personage . . .

A chattering Chinese family pushed past. When they had gone, Charles Smith was crossing the grass towards us. Alone. I heard Su's gasp of dismay. It almost matched my own.

'My friends had to go. They had a previous engagement,' Charles apologised. 'But should you find time to call on us on your way back to Singapore, then I shall arrange a little soirée. You would find them most cultured and delightful people.' He raised his eyebrows questioningly.

I was the one who answered. It seemed ungracious not to.

'Thank you,' I said. 'We should like that very much.'

*   *   *

I see the dayroom windows now. See the people within occupied with their busy little empty tasks, playing cards, watching television, thinking about their next meal. Karen is there. Karen will stop the pictures running in my head. The worst ones of all. If I am quick enough. If . . .

*   *   *

It was well into the afternoon when we left the main road and began to follow the instructions on the sketch map Charles had left us.

We hadn't meant to be so late but it had been a morning of mishaps. There was a disagreement over our bill which delayed us disagreeably. An hour into our journey the car had a puncture and we had to spend a sweaty time changing the wheel. Then my navigation went haywire and we ended in a dusty laterite cul-de-sac in the middle of nowhere.

If we'd believed in such things we'd have thought the omens distinctly inauspicious. As it was we became increasingly snappy with each other.

'You drive,' Su said, exasperated and cross. 'I'll read the map. Honestly, it's so simple. We should have turned off right, not left . . .'

But even she seemed unsure as the roads became narrower, the jungle closed in and the last small *kampong* was left behind.

The sky was overcast. Despite the open windows, the air in the car was close and stifling. The looming forest trees almost touched over the rutted red track the road had become.

'Are you sure this is the right way?' I began, fighting the Pontianak's steering.

'Yes! Look, Rubber trees—and there's the gate.'

Her relief matched my own as jungle was replaced by neatly ordered rows of trees, each trunk bearing the cup into which the latex dripped, like white blood, from the slanting gash in the bark.

We turned between stone gateposts and drove up a metalled road fringed with shaved lawns and clipped shrubs. The house, built in the colonial style of an earlier era, stood on a small rise. Two-storeyed, an almost luminescent white against the heavy, thundery sky, its louvred shutters were opened wide to catch the breeze. It spoke of good order and comfort and good living.

We were smiling with relief as we climbed out of the car, yet something niggled me as I stared round.

'The photograph he showed me. He was standing there.' I pointed to a grassy terrace flanked by stone tubs of flaring canna lilies. 'And his friends—they were there, too. I remember now.' I frowned. 'It wasn't a very good photograph, though. All blurred. It didn't look anything like this. Sort of overgrown. Not nearly so grand.'

But Su wasn't listening, she was already at the open door where Charles Smith waited, glass in hand, to lead us inside.

There were iced fruit drinks laid out on a silver tray in the drawing room. The room was high-ceilinged and cool. Carved blackwood chairs were set round a blue patterned Tientsin carpet.

'You find me rather disorganised,' Charles said. In this elegant, quiet room he seemed more crumpled, more restless, than he had at the Rest House, wandering round us as we perched on the flowered cushions of the chairs sipping the syrupy drinks. Perhaps, too late, he was regretting his invitation to two women who were, after all, practically strangers. 'Crisis in the kitchen, I'm afraid. Cook not too well so I let his missus, the *amah*, trundle him off to the Chinese quack . . .' his voice trailed away. He stared out of the open window at the terraces and lawns and the distant dark rigid rows of the rubber trees.

'We've come at an inconvenient time,' I began, feeling uncomfortable. 'Perhaps we should go . . .'

'No! No!' he said, swiveling round so quickly that his drink lapped over the glass and dripped unnoticed onto the immaculate carpet. 'No, you must stay. Not inconvenient at all.' His restless glance went from me to Su. There was a look of alarm in his doggy little eyes. 'It's all arranged,' he went on more evenly. 'Besides, it's getting late. Dark soon. Storm on its way, wouldn't be surprised.' Then with a touch of gallantry, 'Couldn't let you wander off to face strange roads in a storm. No, no, no. By the time you've had a shower

100

and a rest harmony will be restored in the domestic department. My other friends will be here. Nice little dinner party, eh? Something different. Something . . . of the country. Unusual.'

'Probably fried rice and *gula Malacca*,' Su whispered, wrinkling her nose as we followed Charles up the wide shallow stairs. Her eyes were bright with excitement. 'But I'd willingly eat the Malay version of sago pud, so long as a certain royal charmer's served up with the coffee.'

My stomach heaved at the thought of food. The fruit drink had been far too sweet and sickly. I yawned. 'I'm exhausted. I'll crash out for an hour, I think.'

'Me, too.' Su's face was pale under the freckles and the peeling skin on her nose. 'Hope we've got decent beds . . . My God, not half!' Our rooms were opposite each other on the upstairs corridor. We blinked at them through the open doors. 'I don't believe it! I've got a four poster. And all those bowls of orchids and gardenias. It's like a bower. I haven't strayed into the honeymoon suite by some chance? And the bathroom! It's vast. I'll get lost on the way to the bath.'

Charles smiled, that bland, all-purpose smile. 'I try to make my guests comfortable.' Beads of sweat dewed his upper lip. 'You'll be called . . . when it's time to eat.'

He gave a half bow and retreated down the

corridor.

'He may be an oddball but he must be loaded,' Su said as we wandered round the rooms, fingering ornaments, opening drawers. 'Look at this plate. Famille Verte, do you think? Hey play your cards right and you might land yourself a rich rubber planter.'

I shuddered, rubbing my arm and remembering the touch of those damp fingers. 'Do me a favour.'

Su giggled. 'He is a bit of a wart, isn't he?' She was overpowered by a yawn and flung herself on the lemon silken coverlet of the bed. 'Not like my Prince, eh?'

I think she was asleep before I left the room. I wavered across the corridor and fell blissfully onto my own bed.

*   *   *

The dayroom is warm. I shut the door carefully and lean against it. I move only my eyes. My head feels fragile on my stalk of a neck. The door supports my back. If I move away from it, my rubbery knees will give way. My eyes move, searching frantically for Karen. She's not here. Where are you, you stupid girl? Can't you see . . . ? Don't you know . . . ? I need help. I need . . . need . . .

*   *   *

It was dark when I woke. There had been a sound. 'Su?' I croaked, my throat dry. No answer. I could still taste that sickly fruit juice. Yuck.

I pulled myself upright and groped for the light switch. A reluctant, flickering circle of light spilled over the bedside table, flinging most of the room into a deadly gloom. Grumbling, I rolled off the bed and found the switch for the ceiling light. That didn't work. Power problems, I thought, thick-headed still. Out here they perhaps had to rely on generators. Then I stood still, listening. Was that someone moving in the corridor? Was it time to go to dinner? Had I missed the call? God, I hadn't even showered or changed out of my sweat-soaked shirt and pedal-pushers.

I realised, muzzily, that my door was shut. I didn't remember shutting it. Perhaps the *amah* was back. Perhaps she'd looked in and seen me sleeping and closed the door. I hoped to heaven it hadn't been Charles Smith doing a Peeping Tom act.

I groped my way towards the bathroom. The light, thank heavens, did work in here, if dimly. At least it was enough to see . . .

I sprang back, aware of my bare feet. Sandals, sandals, where? There, by the bed. Shuddering I slipped my feet into them, buckled them up, groped for my suitcase.

Flit spray in hand I crept towards the bathroom. Blast the little horrors. They'd get everywhere. Even in a grandiose bathroom like this, all pink marble surfaces and gleaming tiles.

There were three cockroaches. Big, brown, shiny, hesitating by the drain. I aimed the Flit gun. Fired.

'Gotcha!' I said, watching them flee in a wash of insecticide into the drain. 'Curtains for you, mateys,' I said, grimly satisfied.

There didn't seem to be any others. Gingerly, I edged in the gloomy yellow light to the bath and turned on the taps. I tipped in half a bottle of pink-tinted oil from the cut-glass jar on the shelf and a cloud of scented steam rose from the water.

I was unbuttoning my shirt when I heard a little tinkling sound from the corner by the drain. I turned sharply, my hand reaching automatically for the Flit gun. No cockroaches. I frowned. Odd. A shower of plaster had fallen from the wall under the washbasin. Even as I looked a crack zig-zagged out from the puddle of insecticide—two cracks, more. Fanning out, up through the tiles on the wall, along the terrazzo floor.

With a clatter, a handful of broken tiles fell away from the plaster.

I looked at the pink heap, then back to the wall.

Like some sort of crazy contagion, the fan of cracks kept on growing up the wall, spread across the floor towards my feet.

The Flit gun was suddenly a guilty weight in my sweaty hand. The insecticide. It must be. Some weird effect on the plaster—even on the tiles themselves. I retreated towards the bedroom. How on earth was I going to explain this to Charles Smith?

As I backed away the cracks came with me. They'd reached the bath now, run along the tiled sides, then over into the bath itself. Water began to ooze through in small drips, then big fat trickles. I stared in shock as the cracks raced towards the taps. With a cough and a gurgle, the taps suddenly dried up. They instantly lost their pristine golden gleam, became dull, crumbled rustily to brown powder and fell with a hiss into the remaining water.

It couldn't be happening! The whole of the bathroom was disintegrating before my eyes. Worse, out of the cracks, the gaping holes, swarmed a mess of familiar, loathed bodies. Darting from their crumbling refuge on speedy, energetic legs.

I ran then, banging the door behind me, hearing the clatter of falling, rotting fitments.

'Su!' I screamed. 'Su!'

I wrenched open my bedroom door, flung myself across the black corridor and banged on her door.

I burst in. Blackness again, was she here? Had she already gone downstairs, abandoning me? I found the light switch. Mercifully it worked. Dim, though, a mere yellowing of the darkness. But enough to see . . .

Nightmare.

I was caught in it, trapped in it, part of it.

The air was dense with the smell of flowers and with another, underlying odour that caught at my throat and made me gag.

They were standing at the foot of the bed. Su and the beautiful prince she so desired.

His arms were round her. Her hands were locked round his head, drawing his open mouth down to hers. I saw the dark wet gleam of his tongue the pink, seeking, sensual lips.

'No, Su! No!'

I don't know how I knew or why. It was more sense than sight in that dim light.

I sensed *them*. That smell . . .

A voice in my head, chilling, soothing, calming.

Don't be afraid. She has been chosen. She will give such pleasure.

The woman advanced from the shadows. The tawny oval of her face, the gleam of her lustrous eyes, seemed more perfect in close-up than I could have imagined. I was breathless, paralysed for a second by her beauty, the warmth and closeness of her welcoming smile.

Her hands fluttered out towards me.

Come, my dear. You, too, must play your part. Her voice sank to a whispery throb. In it I seemed to hear music, laughter, a thousand luminous golden delights. *Come to me and do not be afraid.*

I swayed. Lulled, weakened.

But that smell, that foetid odour the scent of the flowers could not disguise . . .

'No!' I gasped.

It was an effort of will to wrench my eyes from hers, to plead once more with Su.

But Su was beyond hearing.

His kiss was upon her.

I saw the cockroaches flow like a brown slithery rushing tide from his mouth to hers, into her, over her, through her tangled red hair, under her clothes. I saw her writhe and jerk and moan in that terrible orgasm, as they sank, locked together, to the floor.

I screamed but she was past hearing.

The woman's mouth gleamed wetly open. I could see the dark heaving in its red depths. So close . . . so tempting . . .

I heaved up the Flit gun, its weight like a cannon in my weakened arms. I pumped it into her face, into her lustrous eyes, into that gaping cavern of a mouth.

Her hands flew up and she fell back. I swung the spray round, poured it onto the seething, bloody mess on the carpet that had been my friend and the giant, gnawing, rutting thing that feasted its lust and its hunger on her.

Then I ran.

Into the corridor. A place of gaping holes and crumbling plaster. Lightning flickered between the rafters open to the sky. Down the rotting stairs, slithering and skidding on things that crunched under my feet. Past that poor wretch, Charles Smith, swaying like an upright corpse amid the ruin below.

'Come back,' he wailed. 'There's no escape. You . . . I . . . will be punished. You were chosen . . .'

The keys to the Pontianak were still in my pocket. Somehow I got into the car, fired the engine. Lightning illuminated the house, fallen in on itself, heavy with creeper, windows like hollow eyes in a skeleton head.

The photograph. That was what I had seen in the photograph.

Perhaps I was not meant to see it. Perhaps it was intended that I should see only the illusion. My inherent fear of those . . . things . . . had momentarily unblinkered my eyes so that I caught an image of dereliction.

I drove like the madwoman I had become. Screaming at the forest that had almost swallowed up the rotten, broken rubber trees, at the storm, at Su, at *them*.

Whoever, whatever they were.

*　　　*　　　*

'There, it's all right, love.' Karen's sympathy flows over me. 'Better now?' I nod. The pictures are fading, dissolving as the sedative takes hold.

'Nobody believed me,' I say, dreamily. 'They

said we'd been ambushed by terrorists. They found Su—what was left of her—months later. Eaten away. Charles Smith lived there once, in that house. Disappeared . . . Japs got him, they said. House a ruin ever since . . .'

'Don't think about it,' Karen says. 'Think about happier things. Like the new place you're going to.'

'No . . . not . . .'

'You'll love it,' she says firmly. 'Much pleasanter than here. It'll be just like being at home. And there's a very nice person come to tell you all about it. One of the team who'll be looking after you. You'll be going to see the house in the morning. Isn't that a nice surprise. Here we are then. Let me introduce you . . .'

'Hi! Nice to meet you at last, Jane.'

His hand locks over mine. He's not a lot different from the others I've met over the years. Dressed in the uniform of the day. Jeans, sweatshirt, earnest smile. Younger than I'd expected. They're all younger than me now. Like policemen. Even him.

'You were older once,' I say, 'when I was young.'

I want to cry, but I laugh instead. Perhaps it's the sedative. Perhaps it's because I'm suddenly tired of running, of fighting.

I feel the damp chill of his clinging fingertips on my hand.

'How many years?' I say. 'Too many for me . . . even worse for you, I think.'

He shakes his head, a look of polite bewilderment masking his face.

'You've lost me there, Jane.'

'You spoke once of punishment,' I say sadly, softly. 'Poor Charles. Poor lost soul. Is eternal youth your punishment or your price? Imprisoned. Made to do their bidding.'

'About tomorrow,' he begins, then hesitates. His bland smile does not reach his restless eyes. I recognize the terror in them that for the moment, dulled by the sedative, lies weightily on my own soul.

'Tomorrow?' I repeat. 'Ah, yes, tomorrow.'

We stand there in silence, hands clasped, like old friends.

And, after a moment, it seems that my head is filled with the soothing sound of a golden voice and the murmur of distant music.

Anne Goring

Mrs Vogel's Ghost. *Woman's Weekly*
 January 2002
Wish Upon a Star. *Weird Tales*. USA 1989
The Party. *Woman's Realm*. June 1982
The Shadow Queen. *The Giant Book of
Fantasy & the Supernatural.* 1994
Hantu Hantu. *Skin of the Soul.* Woman's Press.
1990